THE DOCTOR'S SECOND CHANCE

ALISON ROBERTS

Boldwood

First published in 2006 as *One Night to Wed*. This edition published in Great Britain in 2025 by Boldwood Books Ltd.

Cover Design by Colin Thomas

Cover Images: Colin Thomas

A CIP catalogue record for this book is available from the British Library.

Paperback ISBN 978-1-83617-376-2

Large Print ISBN 978-1-83617-375-5

Hardback ISBN 978-1-83617-374-8

Ebook ISBN 978-1-83617-377-9

Kindle ISBN 978-1-83617-378-6

Audio CD ISBN 978-1-83617-369-4

MP3 CD ISBN 978-1-83617-370-0

Digital audio download ISBN 978-1-83617-372-4

This book is printed on certified sustainable paper. Boldwood Books is dedicated to putting sustainability at the heart of our business. For more information please visit https://www.boldwoodbooks.com/about-us/sustainability/

Boldwood Books Ltd, 23 Bowerdean Street, London, SW6 3TN

www.boldwoodbooks.com

1

It was a most unpleasant sensation.

The hairs on the back of Felicity Slade's neck rose slowly, and the nasty prickle was enough to make her lose concentration on the pulse she could feel beneath her fingertips.

A reflection of her sudden disquiet showed in the faded blue eyes of her elderly patient.

'Something wrong, Fliss?'

There were no words that could convey such a formless fear, and for a split second Fliss simply stared blankly, still caught by that primal and totally unexpected physical reaction to a sense of danger.

Her patient patted her hand. 'Don't look so worried, love. I've been expecting bad news. This old ticker of mine's been on its last legs for years.'

Fliss was mortified. How unprofessional was she being here? Not only had she allowed herself to be totally distracted from her examination, but she had also made one of her favourite patients fear the worst.

'Your pulse feels fine, Jack. Just a little bit faster than normal. I need to have a good listen to the back of your chest now. Can you lean forward a little, please?'

Fliss pulled her stethoscope from where it was hanging around her neck. 'I'm so sorry about that,' she added. 'I just got distracted by the weirdest feeling. Like something was wrong.'

'Something *is* wrong. Why do you think I called you out when you should be having your dinner? My shoes feel too tight and I'm short of puff as soon as I try doing anything.'

'Hmm.' Fliss was happy to concentrate on her consultation again. 'Take some deep breaths for me, Jack.' She could hear some crackles at the base of both lungs. 'Have a good, hard cough for me.'

The fruity sound Jack produced made her shake her head ruefully. 'You haven't cut down on the smoking much, have you?'

Jack's grunt was amused. 'As you well know, my dear, I've been on the fags for more than seventy years. Trying to stop would kill me quicker than anything else is going to.'

There was a distinct twinkle in the gaze that caught hers as Jack twisted his head and the faint Scottish brogue in his voice, which had never quite vanished despite being in a foreign country for a large proportion of those seventy years, grew stronger. 'And you're not going to tell me to get lost just because I still have the odd wee puff, are you?'

'The odd puff?' Fliss had to laugh. 'I reckon you manage twenty a day.' She placed the disk of her stethoscope halfway down Jack's skinny back. 'Let me have another listen now that you've shifted a bit of that muck.'

The crackles were still there, which wasn't unexpected. It fitted with the swelling Jack had in his ankles and his breathlessness on exertion or lying flat.

'I think the chest infection you've had could be making your heart failure a bit worse, Jack,' Fliss told her patient. 'You're accumulating fluid and that's why you're getting that puffiness in your ankles and feet. When the levels go up, it makes your lungs soggy as well – so that's why you're getting short of puff.'

'It's all that water I drink, isn't it?' The long-retired fisherman scratched thoughtfully at the fluffy white beard covering his chin and glared at the old valve radio that took pride of place on his cluttered kitchen table. 'I should never have listened to that so-called expert on the wireless. Eight glasses a day, they said! Should have just stuck with my beer, shouldn't I?'

Fliss widened her eyes. 'You mean to tell me you've been drinking water at the pub every night?'

'Hell's bells, lassie – are you mad? I've been drinking the water *before* I go down to the Hog. It's no bloody wonder I'm waterlogged now, is it? It's going to be the dry dock for me from now on. As far as the water goes, anyway,' he added hastily.

Fliss wrapped a blood-pressure cuff around a still surprisingly muscular upper arm. 'It's got nothing to do with how much water you drink, Jack. If your heart's working as well as it should, the rest of your body can do its job properly, and the only difference eight glasses of water a day will make is in how many times you have to pee.'

Something made Fliss pause again before she pumped up the pressure cuff and put the stethoscope in place. Maybe it was the memory of what she had felt only minutes before. Her senses were still on full alert and the idea of cutting off her ability to hear something important was creating an odd reluctance.

She glanced through the glass doors that made up one side of Jack's kitchen, the side that looked down the hill towards the sea and the river mouth that bordered the tiny coastal settlement on the west coast of New Zealand's South Island.

'Quiet, isn't it?'

A rumble of laughter came from the man sitting beside the scrubbed pine table. 'You've only just noticed?'

Fliss grinned. The peace and quiet were certainly two of the most notable attributes of Morriston. She'd been here for three months now in her position as a locum GP and it *would* seem laughable if she hadn't acclimatised to the ambience. Then her smile faded.

'No, I mean it's quieter than normal.'

Jack swivelled on the spindle-backed wooden chair to join her in staring through the glass. His unpretentious house, which had once been someone's holiday home, was further up the hill than many in the village so the view was one of the best.

They could see one of his closest neighbours, Bernice, across the dusty, unsealed street as she stood in her garden, watering tomato plants. At the bottom of the street, where Fliss would turn right to get to her house that incorporated the small surgery, there were two small boys riding their bicycles in the fading light of a warm spring evening. A couple was walking near the beach with their dog, and right over at the river mouth there was more than one person standing thigh deep in the water, dragging in the big, box-type nets using for catching the local delicacy of whitebait.

'High tide.' Jack nodded. 'Been a bumper season for whitebait so far.'

'Mmm.' Fliss wasn't overly fond of the tiny fish because you could still see their eyes when they had been cooked up in the traditional fritters, but she had to accept the satisfied note in Jack's voice that suggested there was nothing outwardly amiss in the scene.

It was quiet, yes. Peaceful. Picture perfect, in fact. Just the kind of place where Fliss had spent many happy summer holidays as a child. An advertisement for the quintessential security she had sought in order to get through her current life crisis.

With a slow nod, Fliss suppressed that odd feeling of persistent unease and turned back to complete her examination.

'Your blood pressure's down a bit but it's not bad,' she said a minute later. 'I'm going to keep you on those antibiotics for a few more days to make sure we've knocked that chest infection on the head. And I'll take a blood sample now so I can check some other things.' Like whether Jack's increasing level of heart failure was due to a silent heart attack, but Fliss didn't want to alarm Jack unnecessarily.

'I'm going to increase your dose of diuretic as well. Hopefully that will do the trick in getting rid of that excess fluid.' Fliss took a deep breath and ploughed on. 'I'd really like to refer you to a cardiologist, Jack, for a more expert opinion.'

Jack snorted. 'You'll do, lass. Word is that you gave up the offer of a top spot in that emergency department in Christchurch to come over here. Lord knows why, but I reckon I've got all the expertise I need right now.'

'Where on earth did you hear something like that?'

'Word gets around in these parts.'

'Obviously.' The accuracy of the gossip was disconcerting. What else was everybody in Morriston discussing over their jugs of beer? The disaster of her personal life, maybe? The recent, devastating failure in her personal relationships?

The consternation in her tone was enough to make Jack smile reassuringly. 'We only heard good stuff,' he said kindly. 'A mate of mine was in Greymouth hospital for a few days, that's all. One of the doctors there knew about you. He said we were lucky to get someone with your qualifications who didn't mind being stuck out in the sticks.' Jack's smile was smug. 'That's how I know I don't need to go anywhere else for my medical care.'

'I can't give you the best care when I don't know exactly what I'm dealing with, Jack. There are tests they can do which would tell me a lot. Simple things like a chest X-ray and an echocardiogram. You don't have to go all the way to Christchurch or anything. Just down to Greymouth.'

Jack shook his head decisively. 'I've told you, Fliss. Just what I've told all the other doctors that have come and gone in these parts. I haven't crossed the river since I retired and I've got no intention of crossing it now. I'm eighty-six. Nobody lives for ever and when I pop my clogs I intend to do it in the privacy of my own home. Or maybe down at the Hog.'

Fliss sighed. 'Fair enough.'

That the local pub qualified as a second home made her smile. The old stone building near the general store that Mrs McKay ran was far more of a social hub than the pretty church or the memorial hall opposite the doctor's surgery, but Fliss didn't mind. She liked being at the end of the quietest street with plenty of time to soak in the peace and quiet in the hope of unravelling the tangled knots in her head and heart.

Pulling a tourniquet and the items she needed to take a blood sample from her bag, Fliss kept a straight face. 'Which arm today, then?' she queried.

Jack pursed his lips thoughtfully. 'Make it the right one,' he said finally.

The look they shared acknowledged the joke that had forged the bond Fliss had formed so quickly with the very first patient she had treated in Morriston. The query of which arm the patient preferred to have the sample taken from was automatic and it had popped out on that very first consultation, probably due to Fliss still being unsettled.

The fact that Jack only had one arm, thanks to the fishing mishap that had forced his retirement nearly thirty years ago, had made the question a potential insult, but the old man had given it due consideration to save Fliss's tongue-tied embarrassment, and it was thanks to him that she had suddenly felt at home. Even the disturbing reminder of what she'd left behind that came with the Scottish lilt she could hear in her patient's voice could be dealt with. She was in exactly the right place at the right time in her life.

As she tightened the tourniquet and smiled at the memory, Fliss finally shook off that sense of unease and felt herself relax. She would finish this home visit in a few minutes and then hurry back to her surgery where she knew Maria was probably waiting – amongst others. Convinced that her fifth child was going to put in an early appearance, Maria was attending the evening surgery a couple of times a week now for reassurance, while her husband and children did the evening chores on their rather isolated farmlet.

It was then, in that moment of relaxation, that they heard it.

A sharp crack. Loud enough to make the loose glass pane in one of Jack's doors to rattle just a little. Unexpected enough to make Fliss jump and drop the needle she was about to fit to the end of her ten-mil syringe.

'Just as well you weren't about to stick that into me,' Jack muttered.

'Yeah.' The agreement was wholehearted. 'What on earth was that? It sounded like a gun.' Fliss knew her shudder was probably visible. 'I *hate* guns.'

And anything to do with them. Like the danger they represented.

And the way they automatically made her think of Angus.

'Probably a car backfiring,' Jack said casually.

'Hmm.' Fliss reached into her kit for a fresh needle. An unlikely explanation. Her car might be parked out on the dusty street but that was because she could be needed in a hurry some-where else. As a rule, people didn't bother driving cars on this side of the bridge. Once in the village they could easily walk where they needed to go. Or ride bicycles.

'More likely it's those Johnston boys.' Jack was watching Fliss as she ripped open an alcohol swab. 'Guy Fawkes is only a week or so away. They're probably having a test run of their crackers.'

Fliss glanced outside again to where the young Johnston twins had been riding their bikes. Sure enough, two bicycles lay abandoned in the middle of the street, one with its front wheel still spinning slowly. Under one end of the long macrocarpa hedge that bordered the Treffers' property, a pair of short legs could be seen protruding. A small boy hiding, perhaps – avoiding the potential consequences of an illicit act.

The second crack was even louder.

'Now, that *did* sound like a gun,' Jack said. 'Maybe Darren's doing something stupid in his back yard.'

It was quite possible. Darren was a local resident who shot possums in the vast tracts of native bush that cut Morriston off from the Southern Alps. As one of New Zealand's most destruc-tive pests, the culling was commendable but the way Darren left the carcasses piled in his driveway awaiting his taxidermy skills before being sent to the tourist shops was fairly unpopular with his neighbours.

'Mind you,' Jack added when a series of cracks made the windows as well as the doors rattle, 'that's no shotgun he's using.'

Fliss unsnapped the tourniquet as Jack stood up. There was no way she could concentrate on taking a blood sample until they discovered the cause of this disturbing interruption.

They both moved to the glass doors.

'Look!' Fliss pointed towards the river mouth. 'The white-baiters are getting out of the water in a hurry.'

Jack picked up a pair of binoculars from the end of his kitchen bench with an ease that suggested it was an automatic gesture. 'It's those Barrett boys,' he told Fliss.

The fact that the Barrett 'boys' were both well into their fifties failed to raise a smile. She knew the brothers lived well out of the village, worked sporadically at a sawmill down the coast and relied heavily on the whitebait season to supplement their income. Right now, they were wading ashore with a speed that was at complete odds with the impression of laziness Fliss had gained on the one occasion she had met them.

The speed was enough to see one of them stumble and sprawl headlong into the slow-moving water.

'Why have they left their nets behind?'

Jack didn't answer the question. The way his grip on the binoculars tightened was enough to make Fliss catch her breath, and it wasn't just Jack's sudden focus that brought those hairs up again on the back of her neck.

Her eyesight was more than good enough to see that the man who had stumbled wasn't getting up again.

He was floating, face down in the water, while his brother continued his dash to the shore.

'Jack?' The tone was urgent and Fliss took the binoculars that he handed over in stunned silence.

Now Fliss could see something she would never have seen with the naked eye. Something she had not wanted to see.

A dark stain in the water to one side of the floating figure. Quickly dispersed, of course, only to re-form.

'Oh, my God,' Fliss breathed. 'He's been *shot*, hasn't he, Jack?'

'Come away from the window.' Jack took Fliss's elbow in a firm grip and propelled her back into the kitchen, but not before she took a wild visual sweep of the view closer to hand.

The impressions were momentary. Someone was running

past the end of Jack's street. The boys' bicycles still lay in the dust and a small boy's legs could still be seen under the Treffers' hedge. Bernice was nowhere to be seen and the hose she had been using to water the tomatoes lay abandoned, the nozzle twisting gently due to the pressure of its undirected spray.

'What's happening. Jack?'

'I dunno. But whatever it is, I don't like it.' Jack reached for the telephone on the wall beside an interior door. 'I'm calling Blair.'

The local police officer was bound to be at the Hog at this time of day, having a quiet beer and keeping his finger on the pulse of his district. Luckily, he lived in Morriston and not one of the other scattered villages that he shared with Fliss as part of his responsibility. But Jack put the receiver down a moment later and shook his head.

'Line's busy.'

'Call the emergency services,' Fliss instructed. 'We need help.' She swallowed hard. 'Someone needs to rescue that man in the river. He's going to need treatment fast.'

'I reckon it's too late for that,' Jack said heavily.

Neither of them wanted to look towards the river mouth and see if the body was still floating. Neither of them could help themselves.

Jack made a sound of frustration but then shook his head. 'Nobody's going to be crazy enough to wade out there while someone's taking potshots at people.'

'But who would be doing something like that? Why?'

Jack shrugged. 'I've heard rumours about the Barrett boys. I suspect they grow more than veggies up there in the bush.'

'People don't get shot because they grow a bit of cannabis on the side.'

'Don't be too sure. It's big business in these parts and the police chopper operations don't find all the plantations by any means.'

'You think this is deliberate, then? Some kind of patch warfare?'

'Let's hope so.'

Fliss said nothing. Jack was right. The alternative was too horrible to contemplate. Far better that Jack was guessing correctly and there was a specific target that would only endanger innocent people if they got in the way.

Jack had entered the three-digit emergency number into his phone.

'Police,' Fliss heard him request brusquely. Then he said 'Morriston' in response to what had to be a query regarding location. Then he was silent for what seemed an inordinately long time. Finally he nodded.

'Right you are.' The call was disconnected.

'You didn't tell them anything,' Fliss protested.

'Didn't need to. There's an armed offender operation already underway. They got the first call about fifteen minutes ago.'

'But that was before we even heard the first shot.'

'Maybe someone saw something. Or maybe someone was making threats.' He gave Fliss a curious glance. '*You* knew, didn't you? That something wasn't right?'

'I wouldn't have called the police on the strength of a premonition,' Fliss said wryly. 'But at least we know help's on the way.'

'They said to stay put. Not to go outside under any circumstances. They said to lock our doors and windows, keep the lights off and stay hidden. They'll let us know when it's safe to come out.'

'What?' Fliss was horrified. 'I've got patients waiting at the surgery. What if someone's been shot and needs urgent treatment? I can't stay hidden!'

'Yes, you can, lass,' Jack said firmly. 'It's getting dark out there. We have no idea what's going on or where the idiot with the gun is. What use would you be to anyone if you go out there and get shot yourself?'

There were no streetlights in Morriston. When it got dark, it got absolutely dark. It might only be a few hundred metres to the surgery but it would be a long way to travel with the knowledge that any movement could attract the attention of someone with little regard for the law or the sanctity of human life. Even absolute darkness was probably not enough cover for someone with bright blonde hair like Fliss's – especially when she was wearing a white shirt over her jeans.

'I've got a cellar,' Jack told her. 'Damp little hole carved into the hill that's been no use for storage so it's empty. Won't be that comfortable but it'll be safe enough. You can come out and do your bit to help when the police arrive and you've got some protection.'

The notion of hiding was undeniably attractive. Fliss was good at hiding. It was why she had come to Morriston in the first place, wasn't it? To hide from the painful reminders of what could have been if only things had been different.

Fliss had achieved the isolation she'd sought, but how ironic was it that she was now in a situation in which she needed Angus more than she had ever needed anyone?

Or that the reason she needed him so badly was the very reason that had forced her to end the relationship? Angus knew what it was like to face danger like this. He had the training and skills to deal with it. To protect himself and others.

But he was hundreds of miles away in Christchurch. Would SERT – the specialist emergency response team – be activated in response to an armed offender callout in Morriston?

Probably. They got sent to any kind of hotspot that needed police and paramedic personnel.

Would Angus be on duty?

Fliss didn't know. She had worked hard to try and stop thinking about him all the time. To stop imagining what he might be doing on a particular day or at a particular time of day or night. To stop wondering whether he had got over being furious to find he missed her as much as she missed him.

Success in her endeavours had been patchy. Fliss still thought about Angus far too often for her peace of mind, but she had forgotten his roster.

If he came, dressed in operational gear like his armed police team members, the sanctuary Fliss had found would be gone. Morriston, as much as Christchurch, would remind her of Angus. Of the direction his career as a paramedic had taken him. Of its call to put him in dangerous places and situations that had the potential to claim his life. A potential that had spelt the end of a future together as far as Fliss had been concerned.

But the safety of Morriston was already violated, wasn't it? Fliss had never been this afraid in her life. It wouldn't matter if Angus was still furious with her for the way she had ended things. It wouldn't matter if she only saw him for a moment or two in the distance. Just knowing he was nearby would give her the strength to do what she knew she had to do.

Something that could in no way include the safety of Jack's underground cellar.

* * *

The Iroquois helicopter ferrying the personnel equipped to contain and deal with whatever the situation evolving in Morriston could produce was being buffeted by strong wind gusts as it crossed the island's spine of the Southern Alps near the Lewis Pass.

The majority of people on board were part of the special operations squad – an elite division of the police force. Only two of the men were specially trained paramedics whose training crossed the boundaries between police and ambulance. One of those medically qualified SERT members on board the helicopter was Angus McBride.

He nudged the man sitting closest to him and leaned in to be heard above the engine noise.

'Do you think this is for real?'

His partner, Tom, shrugged eloquently. Then he grinned and Angus could hear the message as clearly as if it had been shouted. If the early and somewhat hysterical calls to Police Control were to be believed, there was definitely some kind of battle going on in the sleepy seaside settlement of Morriston.

It sounded like more than one person was armed and dangerous. More than one victim had already been targeted or caught in the crossfire and whoever the perpetrators were, they were not likely to simply give themselves up to the police.

The squad on board this helicopter was heading into unfamiliar and hostile territory and additional resources in the way of manpower or equipment were not going to be readily available. This could well prove to be the biggest challenge he and Tom had faced since joining SERT.

So why wasn't Angus experiencing the same adrenaline rush that Tom's grin had advertised?

Because Morriston was the destination, of course.

Angus leaned close to his partner again. 'Want to know something weird? I was planning to visit Morriston in the next week or two.'

Tom's eyebrows disappeared into the black balaclava covering his head. 'What on earth for?'

Good question. Angus hadn't even told his best mate that he'd finally got over himself and made enquiries at the emergency department of Christchurch's biggest hospital in order to find out exactly where Fliss had taken herself off to when she'd walked out of his life.

Would he really have followed through on his intention to go and see her? To risk rejection again if she was still happy with the way things now were?

It no longer mattered. It didn't matter that the thrill of a big job unfolding had failed to capture Angus. The only thing uppermost in his mind was fear, and the notion of shining a torch on that fear and making it shrink by exposure was too tempting to resist.

'Fliss is there.'

It seemed incongruous to be shouting something that touched such a private part of his soul, but there was no danger of anyone other than Tom hearing. And he was the only one who would recognise the significance of the statement. He deserved to know that Angus had a personal agenda on this job. And Tom would know exactly how significant that agenda might be. He'd seen how devastating it had been to have Fliss walk out like that. He'd had to work with Angus in the weeks when despair and anger had vied for a controlling position in mood determination.

'No way!' Tom looked shocked. 'I thought you said she'd gone up north.'

'I thought she had. I never bothered asking for a specific forwarding address until a few days ago.'

'Why the hell would she go to a place like Morriston?'

'Guess she wanted something a bit different.'

Tom shook his head. 'That's not different. It's a total cop-out.' He glanced at Angus. 'You sure she's there right now?'

'As far as I know.'

'You worried, mate?'

Angus couldn't say anything. He could only set his lips into a grim line and look away from the concern on Tom's face.

Of course he was worried.

Worried sick.

Why hadn't he tried earlier to find Fliss? To contact her? To see if he could find a way to persuade her to come home?

To arrive like this wasn't going to help anything. His bullet-proof vest and dark camouflage clothing would only remind Fliss of why she had left in the first place.

But that didn't actually matter right now. The need to find and protect the only woman he had ever truly loved was an issue quite separate from the possibility of them ever getting back together. It was simply something that Angus had to do.

He clenched his fists, urging the helicopter on into the black night. Not that willpower was going to make them get there any quicker, but at least it felt like he was doing *something*.

Before it was too late.

ALISON ROBERTS

2

Even important decisions could sometimes be made purely by default.

Fliss knew she couldn't, in all conscience, choose to stay safely hidden, but the sporadic sound of continuing gunfire made her postpone any move from the relative safety of Jack's now darkened kitchen.

She sat on the floor near the interior door and Jack sat beside her just under the telephone. Waiting for the next, still shocking, evidence of what was going on outside, they strained to hear anything that might warn of danger getting too close.

And in the eerie waiting silence between gunshots, Fliss was all too aware of the sound of Jack's breathing. It sounded worse than it had when she had arrived for her home visit but that was hardly surprising, given the level of stress they had both been plunged into.

'Where are your pills, Jack?'

'On the windowsill. Just above the electric kettle. That way I remember to take them when I make a cuppa, first thing.'

'Did you take one this morning?'

'Yep.'

'I want you to take another one now,' Fliss instructed. 'I'll get it for you.'

But she found a hand on her elbow, dragging her back to the floor as soon as she tried to get to her feet.

'You stay right where you are, lass. I'll get it for myself.'

With a grunt that revealed the effort involved, Jack pushed himself slowly upright. With the ease of familiarity, he negotiated a route past the spindle-backed chairs towards the bench more successfully than Fliss would have managed, but a chair got nudged and scraped on the wooden floorboards all the same. Fliss felt her heart skip a beat and then start to race alarmingly.

She forced herself to take a deep breath in through her nose. And then she let it out slowly.

There was no avoiding the situation they were in. Somehow she had to get a grip on herself and deal with it or she would be no use to anyone, including herself. The notion that she might be paralysed by a panic attack was almost as abhorrent as the violence going on in Morriston.

She was *not* like her mother. She was not about to choose to become a victim – of her own emotions or anyone else's behaviour.

'Jack?'

'Yep?'

'Do you keep your spray with your pills?'

'You mean that stuff for if I get chest pain?'

'Yes.'

'Don't need it.'

'It's not just for angina, Jack. It might help quite a bit with that breathlessness you've got at the moment.' Jack's blood pressure had been high enough to tolerate the potential lowering effect nitrates could have. 'I want you to take two sprays under your tongue.'

'Hmmph!' She could hear Jack shaking a container of tablets. 'I'll take the extra pill and see how I go.'

'No. Take the spray.' Fliss scrambled upright. 'I'm going to have to go down to my surgery, Jack. I don't want to be worrying about you getting worse while I'm gone.'

The lid of the plastic container hit the bench with a rattle. 'You're not going out there!'

'I *have* to, Jack!' Fliss straightened her back to reinforce the determination in her tone. 'You know how we saw one of the Johnston twins hiding under that bush? What if he's not hiding?' Concern tightened her voice. 'What if he's hurt and needs help but he's too scared to go looking for someone?'

Fliss gulped in some air. 'And where's his brother? And what if Maria's waiting for me and she's terrified and she goes into labour? And what about Mr—'

Jack held up his hand. 'All right, pet, I get the message.' He stared at Fliss through the gloom of the unlit room. 'But there's no way I'm going to let you go by yourself. I'm coming with you.'

An eighty-six-year-old with one arm and heart failure as her protector? Fliss almost smiled but had to blink back tears instead. This old man really cared about her safety, and she'd almost forgotten what it was like to have someone really care about *her*. Maybe she couldn't have the man she needed by her side right now, but Jack was better than nothing. A whole lot better than nothing.

'Let's go, then,' Fliss urged. *Now*, she added silently, while she had enough courage gathered to turn her back on personal safety.

'Wait.' Jack scratched his beard thoughtfully. 'You can't go outside like that.'

'Like what?'

'All white and... kind of glowing. That pretty hair of yours would catch anybody's eye.'

Fliss did smile now. 'Is that a compliment, Jack? Why, thank you!'

Jack made a dismissive growling sound. 'If you're mad enough to want to go out there I can't stop you, but you need to cover up. I've got a black hat somewhere. And maybe a jersey or two.'

'You'll need a hat yourself. Your hair's paler than mine.'

'What's left of it.' Jack ran his hand over his balding scalp. Then he smiled at Fliss. 'Guess I've compensated by growing fluff on my chin instead, haven't I?' He didn't wait for a response. 'I've got some old fishing gear out the back. I'll see what I can find.'

'Have you taken that pill yet?'

'Yes.'

'And the spray?'

Grumbling, Jack reached for the small red GTN cannister. 'Bossy, aren't you?'

'I can be.' Fliss nodded. 'But only when I care about what happens to the people I'm bossing.'

She should use any skills in that department to try and make her patient heed police advice and stay in his own home, Fliss decided in Jack's absence. Justifying the danger he was prepared to face with the rationale that she would be able to take better care of his current condition by having him with her at the surgery wasn't good enough.

When Jack returned with an armload of dark clothing, Fliss was ready with her sternest tone.

'I can go by myself, Jack. I'd much rather you stayed here.'

'Not on your nelly.' Jack sounded affronted. 'I'll make my own decisions about some things, missy. You can't *always* get what you want by being bossy, you know.'

Too true.

Jack's reprimand hit a nerve. Angus had considered Fliss to be bossy as well. Stubborn. Uncompromising. The expression 'control freak' had surfaced more than once in the escalating arguments that had marred their last few weeks together.

Did she try and use a position of authority for selfish motives? Had her bossiness really been due to the degree to which she had cared about Angus or had she been more concerned about her personal welfare? Getting what *she* wanted? Had her training as a doctor, in fact, given her a mistaken belief that she could make choices for others that went beyond medical assistance?

Fliss was silent, mulling over what she suspected might be an unpleasant home truth as she pulled on a well-worn woollen pullover in a navy-blue fisherman's rib. Jack was struggling into a similar garment and he rolled up the surplus sleeve and tucked it inside the armhole.

'Blessed nuisance, having two sleeves on everything,' he muttered. 'Nobody caters for the minorities.'

Fliss smiled briefly at the joke as she took the black knitted beanie Jack handed her. These clothes had to be more than thirty years old – relics from Jack's career as a fisherman – and she could almost smell salt-laden air and the tang of fish.

Jack scrutinised the finished result but shook his head sadly. 'It's no good,' he announced.

'Why not?' Fliss jammed the last strands of her shoulder-length wavy hair under the hat. Then she rolled up the sleeves of the oversized jersey so that her hands were free. 'I think it's great. We're both going to be hard to see if we stick to the shadows.'

'Your face is too pale. Let me think...'

Jack actually seemed to be enjoying himself, Fliss realised with astonishment. His breathing sounded less laboured and he

moved more quickly than she had ever seen him when he turned
and headed for his pantry.

'I've got just the thing,' he called over his shoulder. 'You wait
right here.' Fliss peered at the small round tin in his hand when
he reappeared moments later.

'Boot polish?'

'Don't knock it till you've tried it. It's what those top-notch
police fellows use when they go out on dangerous missions.'

'They don't use boot polish, Jack.'

'How would you know?'

'Because I just do. I... used to know some of those police
fellows.'

'Hmmph.' Jack held out the tin. 'Same difference, in any case.
Take the lid off this so I can smear a bit on your face.'

Fliss couldn't resist muttering something about her not being
the only bossy one, but then she stood still as Jack wiped polish
on her face. She returned the favour, blackening Jack's beard as
well as his cheeks. The task suddenly struck her as being ridiculous. Here they were, dressing up like small boys preparing to go
and play some kind of war game. What would Angus say if he
could see her now?

He'd probably laugh. And say something like *Can't beat 'em so
you're going to join 'em, huh? Cool. Come out and play with us, then.*

Except this wasn't any kind of a game. It was real. And deadly.

And Angus, if he was in any way involved tonight, would be
even more effectively camouflaged. Fliss could be quite certain
that he wouldn't be laughing.

'We'll go out the back way,' Jack decided. 'If we go to the top of
the hill and then cut back through the Bennies' orchard, go
through the back of the cemetery and then over the Carsons'
fence, we'll be just about at your place.'

'But if we go that way, we won't go past the Treffers' place. I need to know whether it's Callum or Cody under that bush, Jack. And whether they're okay.'

Jack shook his head. 'It's too exposed. Too risky. If we go my way, we've got more chance of staying hidden.'

By tacit consent, they both edged towards the glass doors to see if staring into the dark street could help finalise their plan of action.

'Look.' For the second time that evening, Fliss pointed towards the river mouth.

On the other side of the bridge, flashing lights could be seen. The red, blue and white lights on the different emergency services vehicles looked like a strobe lighting effect for a large outdoor party.

'The cavalry's arriving.' Jack sounded relieved. 'And it's been less than an hour since all this started. Not bad.'

'But they're not moving. They're miles away.'

'They're not going to let anyone come in until they know it's safe. And they won't want anyone escaping, either. I'll bet they've blocked the road on the north side as well.'

They may as well still be as far away as they had been in the larger towns they had rushed here from, Fliss thought in despair. Relief at knowing help was close was minimised by the frustration of knowing they were still alone on this side of the river.

More lights could now be seen flashing in the sky above the position that had clearly been chosen as a safe rendezvous point. A helicopter was hovering over what had to be Morriston's Domain – a rather grand name for what was little more than a paddock ringed with some lovely old oak trees and used more as a venue for the local pony club to meet than anything else.

Reinforcements from Christchurch?

Would Angus be amongst them?

And if so, how long would he have to wait, cut off by the wide stretch of the Morris River, before he could come to help any of the residents?

To help *her*?

Fliss pushed the selfish thought aside and turned to look away from the tantalising sight of the gathering rescue forces.

The northern boundary of Morriston was hidden from view by the hill Jack's house was on but Fliss looked in that direction anyway. Was the old man right? Had the first priority been to try and seal them off from the outside world to prevent anyone creating mayhem somewhere else? And what about the native bush on the eastern boundary? It would be easy for someone to hide in there for as long as they wanted and then return if they didn't consider the job finished.

An explosion too loud to be gunfire sounded as though it came from just beyond Jack's front doorstep. Fliss instinctively crouched, just as a shower of bright sparks appeared in the inky blackness outside.

Jack remained standing.

'What's happening?' Fliss queried shakily.

'There's a fire.' Jack sounded shocked. 'A big one. I think it might be Darren's house.'

Fliss inched back up to where she could see the first lick of tall flames dividing the sparks. Thick smoke roiled into the night, illuminated by the flames.

Would the volunteer fire brigade dare to respond? Fliss had seen them in action once in her time here, when Mrs McKay's bonfire had spread to a stand of gum trees at the back of her section. A siren had summoned the volunteers, and the ancient vehicle they used had been in place in a commendably short space of time. Rural communities had to look after themselves in that sort of crisis and deal with any type of fire as quickly as possible. Backup would be a long way away if an uncontrolled fire began spreading from tree to tree and then house to house.

But no siren sounded now. If it was Darren's house going up in smoke, it was being left to suffer its fate. 'Whoever lit that fire can't be far away.'

'No.'

'What's going to happen next?'

As if to answer her frightened question, Fliss heard a faint scream from somewhere down the hill.

Then the sound of yet another gunshot.

And then silence.

She looked at Jack.

'I'm going now,' she said quietly. 'I can't just sit here and let this happen.'

'No.' Jack moved, heading for the passage that led to his back door. He opened it, stared for a long moment into the dark section and then jerked his head sideways. 'Right then. Let's go.'

Fliss followed close behind, crouching as she ran. They stopped when they reached the henhouse and huddled into the darkness between the corrugated-iron shed and an overhanging apple tree.

'You go the way I told you, Fliss, and for God's sake, keep a careful lookout and your head down.'

'What are you going to do?' Fliss didn't want to set off alone. Jack might have been eighty-six and in no shape for physical exertion, but doing this alone was a terrifying prospect.

'I'm going past the Treffers' place. I'll check on Callum. Or Cody.' Jack's teeth gleamed oddly in the frame of his blackened beard as he grinned at Fliss. 'Not that I've ever been able to tell those rascals apart. They never get close enough.'

There was an unmistakable undertone of sadness and Fliss knew why it was there. It had taken time, but she had learned that Jack was something of an outsider in this village despite having lived here for most of his adult life. She didn't think he had been a loner by choice, however. While making notes in that very first interview, Fliss had casually queried Jack's marital status. Avoiding her gaze, Jack had been brusque.

'I was always a bit shy when it came to the lassies. And it's a bit late now.'

Perhaps his disfigurement, added to too many years of living alone, had combined to push him further away from the community as he had started to look more disreputable, and the only place he went to socially was the local pub. He didn't have to be alone right now, however. Fliss leaned closer.

'I'll come with you.'

'No.' The gleam vanished. 'It's a more dangerous way to go, Fliss, and you're the important one here. As you said, there could well be people waiting at the surgery who need you.' His hand gripped her shoulder for a second. 'You'll be okay. Just go quietly and carefully.'

'You too, Jack.'

'I'll meet you at your place.'

Fliss simply nodded in response and she couldn't be sure that Jack had noticed. In another moment he was gone. Swallowed up in the night with any sounds of his shuffling movements covered by the soft scratching and clucking from the hens in the run attached to the shed.

Fliss felt very, very alone.

And very, very frightened.

A wave of longing swept over her, so powerful it was a physical pain that tightened her chest and made it hard to draw the deep breath she needed for courage.

She so badly needed to be held right now. By someone who loved her. Someone *she* loved.

No. Not just someone.

Angus.

* * *

The wait seemed interminable.

They were dressed and ready to go.

Angus had been wearing the heavy bullet-proof vest long enough for a familiar knot to be present between his shoulder blades. On top of that was a jacket with pockets everywhere. His police companions used the pockets to carry things like spare ammunition, teargas and stun grenades. Angus had a gas mask in one pocket but the others were bulging with emergency medical supplies. A mini-tracheostomy kit, dressings and bandages to hopefully deal with life-threatening bleeding in the field, some IV gear and drugs.

He wore the headset radio that enabled hands-free communication between all members of the team and he had pulled on a black balaclava and a pair of gloves to complete the uniform. His face was darkened with camouflage crayon and, surrounded by identical figures, the quickest way to spot Tom was to look for the only other man who did not have a revolver on his hip and a larger automatic weapon slung over one shoulder.

Police dogs strained at their leashes and whined softly behind the group, but Angus concentrated on what their operation commander was saying, silently willing him to hurry. To deploy them to the other side of the river where he could find out whether Fliss was safe.

'The offender – or offenders, as we suspect is the case – are not to be shot,' they were reminded. 'Unless they have been called on to surrender and have refused to do so or it is clear it won't be possible to disarm and arrest them without immobilisation and that any delay in apprehending them would endanger others.'

At least that wasn't a call Angus was going to have to make. His job was to provide medical backup to his team members, any victims or even the offender. He would have an armed officer by his side, as would Tom, so they were about to be separated. The township and surrounding areas of Morriston had been divided into sections on paper and colour coded. The squad would be sent to try and cover as much of the area as possible, and the first priority was to locate any of the offenders and contain them.

They still had no idea where the armed offenders were located or how many there were, despite helpful information from the local police officer, Blair, and a resident who had fled the township at the first sign of trouble.

The woman, a Mrs McKay, was still standing nearby with a blanket draped over her shoulders and an ambulance officer close beside her.

'I knew something was going to happen,' Angus had heard her say to his commanding officer just before their briefing. 'Never seen them before and they came into my shop like they owned it. Said they were mates of Darren Blythe and wanted to know where he lived.'

Darren, according to Blair, was on bail. He'd been arrested and charged with the possession of an illegal substance only days ago and it had become evident that he was selling cannabis on behalf of the Barrett brothers.

Whether the older men were cultivating a commercial supply themselves had been something Blair had intended to investigate, but it now seemed likely that they had, in fact, been helping themselves to a crop being carefully nurtured by an out-of-town syndicate using the native bush as cover for a large-scale operation.

'They've all gone too far to be able to back down,' the police chief inspector reminded the squad. 'The firing of weapons has been indiscriminate and we have an unknown number of casualties out there. A greater number of residents are still in their own homes and in danger, but we can't start evacuation until we know where the offenders are located.'

And that could be impossible to find out, given the area that needed clearing and the total lack of light. The house fire that had started maybe ten or fifteen minutes ago stood out like a huge beacon and had the effect of making everything else look far darker. No lights showed in any of the dwellings.

It was all ominously black.

And very quiet.

Terrified people were hiding in these scattered houses.

And one of them was Felicity Slade.

It was an enormous relief when the briefing finally finished. A large police van, with no lights, was used to move the squad across the bridge, where it parked with its rear doors close to the side wall of the general store. The location and lack of windows in Mrs McKay's establishment made it an ideal base for the police operation, and heavy shrubbery that bordered the adjacent small car park afforded cover to those members of the squad who silently melted into the blackness. They dispersed in single units and pairs to make their way to their allocated sectors.

Angus and his police companion, Seth, were going to Green Sector, which covered a street that contained a church, memorial hall, several houses and the doctor's surgery. It was neither coincidence nor a personal request that had landed Angus what would have been a chosen destination. As he was unable to carry anything other than very limited gear, the facility of the community's medical centre could well be needed.

Only Tom knew the relief Angus experienced at having been

handed the opportunity to check on the whereabouts and safety of his ex-partner at such an early stage of an operation that could easily not be resolved until daylight.

It was not something Angus was about to share with anyone else, including Seth. He owed it to his partner to remain as focused as humanly possible on the immediate task they had.

He followed Seth. Very slowly. Moving from one safely sheltered spot to the next, only after waiting and watching long enough to lessen the risk that they weren't alone.

It wasn't just the offenders that they had to worry about, either. The possibility that some residents had been able to arm themselves and were ready to protect their lives and property was very real. A shadowy black figure moving past their hedge or garden shed would appear terrifying. It could well be too late by the time they could identify themselves as the good guys, so they needed to remain hidden from anyone as far as possible.

For the same reason, they would have to treat anyone they encountered with the same kind of caution. Staying in one place would have created tension. Moving towards an unknown destination in foreign territory made it almost unbearable.

* * *

It seemed to be taking forever to get back to what now felt like safety – being within four walls and behind a locked door.

Fliss crept between hiding places and every time she moved just a few metres, she had to crouch and wait until her heart stopped hammering and her breathing slowed so that she could actually hear more than the blood pounding in her head.

Then she would wait, listening intently for anything that might indicate danger. The Bennies' unkempt orchard, with its long grass and overgrown apple trees whose branches mingled with each other, provided reasonable cover, but the black tree trunks and twisted branches looked like stationary figures. It was also a haven for wild creatures, and Fliss broke out in a sweat at the rustling a nearby hedgehog made.

Having reached the end of the orchard, there was a far more daunting space to cross: the tiny cemetery with its headstones casting pools of black shadows so dark they looked like deep water-filled holes. Fliss had never realised how many shades of black existed, and they all seemed threatening tonight.

It took a long time to gather her courage for the next step of this journey, and in those lonely moments Fliss stared at the gravestones and tried not to think of the times she had attended burial services. Of the desolation she'd experienced as a ten-year-old child, watching her father being laid to rest.

Of the guilt and helplessness when she'd stood at her mother's graveside only a few years later.

Fliss might never have found the courage she needed to move into the cemetery if she hadn't heard the faint call.

'Help... Please... Someone help me!'

A woman's voice. A woman who was in pain and terrified. Possibly the one Fliss and Jack had heard scream what seemed like hours before.

Fliss couldn't not respond to the plea for help. The part of her that could forget anything personal and focus totally on the needs of someone else took over, and when she moved this time it was with a confidence and stealth she had been all too aware of lacking up till now.

She almost made it to the crumpled figure lying between a tall headstone and the marble angel that was so old its nose had crumbled off. But by the time she saw the black figure launch itself at her from the shadow of another headstone, it was far too late to even turn, let alone try to flee or defend herself.

She landed in the grass, face down, with a jolt that forced any air out of her lungs, and the pain of trying to breathe again almost overwhelmed the fear that came with the knowledge that she was about to die.

It was a male figure pinning her to the ground. No woman could weigh that much and still have the feel of iron-clad muscle and untold strength. Why hadn't he shot her, like the others? Had he finally run out of ammunition? Was he going to kill her by some much slower and therefore more horrendous method?

Fear kicked in then, and Fliss struggled, ready to fight for her life.

She felt herself turning onto her back, but her arms were pinned to the ground on either side of her head and her legs were still crushed by the weight of her attacker.

The struggle was silent and fierce. The paralysing effect on her diaphragm from the initial body blow meant that Fliss couldn't draw enough breath to scream yet. When she found she could suck in some oxygen, she stopped struggling for a split second to do just that.

And in that moment, she focused on the face hovering so close to her own. She could see the features that were well disguised but not altered by the black substance that covered them.

Could see dark eyes that were staring back at her with an extraordinary expression.

A strangled sound like a sob finally escaped Fliss. A release of terror. The birth of something far more welcome.

Her hoarse whisper was a desperate plea to confirm what she thought she was seeing.

'Angus?'

3

'*Shh!*' Angus laid a gloved finger on her lips, with just enough pressure to remind Fliss that they could both be in danger right now.

He raised his head and gave a curt nod, as though responding to an unseen message from someone else.

'Okay,' he whispered, removing his finger. 'We're covered. But keep very still, Fliss, and speak very quietly.'

She simply nodded, still trying to take in the fact that Angus was here. It hadn't felt exactly like protection, though, had it? Being tackled like that and hurled to the ground.

'I thought you were *him*,' she whispered, a long moment later. 'That you were going to kill me.'

A gleam in the dark face showed as Angus smiled. 'Same.' His head moved as he scanned the woman he was still lying half on top of. 'Are you hurt, Fliss?'

'No. I'm fine. Just... scared.'

'I know.' Angus was still staring at her. 'Why are you dressed like *this*?'

'It was Jack's idea.'

'Jack? Who the hell is Jack?'

Fliss could feel something remarkably like a smile gathering somewhere deep inside her. Despite this conversation being rapid-fire and quiet enough to be almost inaudible, she could detect something that sounded astonishingly like jealousy in that question.

Did Angus still care?

He clearly cared enough to want to protect her, and that was enough for the moment. He was still shielding her body with his own, and Fliss couldn't help her awareness of the familiar feel of his long legs over hers. Of his lower body in close contact with her own. It imparted a sense of security that was so incongruous to the setting it was confusing. And perhaps it was that odd sense of security that allowed something in Fliss to respond so acutely to hearing that soft lilt underlying the deep voice. To remember things that gave her a tingling down her spine that had far more to do with excitement than fear.

'He's a patient,' Fliss murmured. 'I was at his house when this started. We're trying to get back to my surgery.'

She could feel the new tension in Angus's body as his level of alertness suddenly increased.

'Where is he now?'

'He went a different way. There's a little boy who might be hurt.'

The low moan from nearby reminded Fliss of a more urgent mission. Of someone who was definitely hurt.

'There's someone here!' Fliss couldn't stop her voice getting louder. 'I was trying to get to her when you attacked me.'

'I was heading for her myself,' Angus responded. 'And then I spotted you.' He rolled sideways and Fliss sat up. Angus pulled her flat again instantly.

'Wait,' he commanded. 'I'll go first.' He raised his hand and made some sort of signal.

'What are you doing?'

'Letting Seth know what the plan is. We don't use our radios unless we have to.'

'Seth?'

'My partner. He's armed and close. He's going to cover me while I check out that woman.'

Fliss stared around her but could see nothing. Then she stared harder. A pinprick of red light showed behind a gravestone that was only a few metres away.

'That light...?'

'Sights on the gun.'

Good grief! Someone was pointing a weapon right at them at almost point-blank range, and Fliss had had no idea he was even there. These guys were good at what they did and no mistake. She was quite happy to let Angus be the one to move and see what the situation was with the groaning woman.

The sound of distress grew louder a few seconds later.

'It's my leg,' Fliss heard the woman say hoarsely. 'I can't move.'

'*Shh.*' Angus spoke too quietly for Fliss to catch any words, but she could sense the reassurance in whatever he was saying. When the woman spoke again, she copied his inaudible volume.

Long seconds of silence ensued and then a louder groan followed by an apology from his patient. Angus must be doing something that had increased her pain temporarily, Fliss thought. A rough splint, perhaps, or inserting an IV line.

She saw one of the dark shapes move and a moment later Angus was back beside her.

'She's been shot in the leg. It's fractured her femur and there's been heavy blood loss. I've got a dressing and pressure bandage on it and I've given her some pain relief, but she's in shock. How far from your surgery are we?'

'Not far.' Fliss matched his whisper. 'I was going to climb over the Carsons' fence there to get to the street. My place is two houses down from there.'

'I'm going to carry Maria.'

'Maria?' Fliss was shocked. 'What was she doing here?'

'Hiding, I expect. She's not too big so I can carry her, but not over a fence.'

'She's pregnant,' Fliss told him. 'Thirty-six weeks.'

'I did notice.' Even the whisper sounded wry.

'Her babies have come a bit earlier each time. This is number five.'

'Definitely not over a fence, then.'

There was an undercurrent of amusement in the whisper now. And something else. A response to a challenge? Excitement, even?

'I'm going to have a word with Seth. We might need some extra cover so we can go down the street.'

The consultation with the still unseen Seth took less than a minute. Then they waited for perhaps another ten minutes until they were given permission to carry out the planned rescue mission. Angus went back to Maria, but Fliss was ordered to stay where she was for the moment. It was a long time to sit in silence, knowing that every minute could represent a deterioration in their patient's condition.

She needs oxygen, Fliss thought. And fluids. Being in shock would be a danger to the baby, whose survival depended on the oxygen supply it received from its mother's blood.

Maria adored her children and after four girls she was convinced that a longed-for boy was due to arrive. Fliss had visited their alternative lifestyle block where they grew most of their own food and home-schooled their children. She had envied the contentment and solidarity of the self-sufficient family. She couldn't let anything horrible happen to Maria *or* the baby.

The wave of anger towards the perpetrator of this violence shouldn't have come as such a surprise to Fliss. It was people like that who shattered the lives of innocent people, including children.

The way hers had been shattered all those years ago. Sitting in the cemetery with the memories of her own losses made Fliss all too aware of what the repercussions of random acts of violence like this could be. The effects could be so far-reaching they could interfere with the rest of your life. They could put what you wanted more than anything out of reach. Could undermine and destroy relationships.

As hers had been.

The force that had plucked her father from her life had not been something a person could be blamed for because no one had ever been caught for the arson attack that had started the house fire. That her firefighter father had been caught when the roof had collapsed unexpectedly had been deemed a disastrous miscalculation. A terrible accident but one that came with the territory of such a career.

Some of her earliest memories had to do with that nebulous force of danger that had hung over her father's career, reinforced by her mother's anxiety every time he'd gone on duty. For the first time, however, Fliss could feel hatred for the person who'd committed the mindless act of starting that fire in the first place. The same kind of hatred she was experiencing towards whoever was roaming through Morriston right now with a loaded gun.

And she could find an outlet for such a negative emotion much closer to hand. In the men who chose a career that brought them close to that kind of evil. Who waited for it to happen.

Looked forward to it, even, because it provided excitement. When Angus came back to her position, Fliss found herself watching for evidence of that career satisfaction.

'You guys are enjoying this, aren't you?'

'Keep your voice down, Fliss.'

'This must be the biggest callout you've ever had.'

'*Shh!*' The hiss was a command. 'We're moving. Follow me, and for God's sake, shut up.'

Fliss complied, her anger replaced by fear. Angus gathered Maria into his arms seemingly effortlessly and Fliss walked beside him with Seth on her other side. She presumed they had cover from other members of the squad, although she couldn't see anyone.

Maria bravely kept as silent as she could, her pale face pressed into Angus's shoulder, her broken leg hidden by the long, flowered dress she wore. The ungainly knot of humanity crept slowly along the street until Fliss breathed an audible sigh of relief.

'This is it. My surgery.'

A faded sign designated the add-on to the small cottage as the 'Morriston Medical Centre'. Fliss had left her keys with the rather cumbersome kit back at Jack's house, but it didn't matter. The door, panelled with opaque glass, that led into the small waiting room was never locked. Fliss reached for the handle.

'Wait!'

'Why?'

'Has this door been unlocked since you left?'

'Yes. I never lock it on Wednesdays. I usually hold surgery hours between seven and nine and if I'm called out, people need somewhere to wait.'

Seth and Angus exchanged a glance and Fliss dropped her hand. What if someone was waiting inside who wasn't a patient?

It had never occurred to her that she needed to fret about security in a place like Morriston.

Things were never going to be the same after this.

'I'll check it out,' Seth said quietly. 'Stay here.'

He was back only moments later. There hadn't been much to check. A waiting area, a toilet, the consultation room and a small storage space. The connecting interior door that led from the waiting area into the cottage was always locked from the house side. If Fliss wanted to enter her home during working hours, she would walk around the corner to the small veranda that had her front door exactly in the middle.

Angus carried Maria straight into the consultation room and laid her gently on the bed. Seth locked the outside door behind them and then pulled the curtains closed.

'Don't turn on any more lights than you absolutely have to,' he instructed.

Fliss put a desk lamp on the floor, angled the head down and switched it on. The pool of light wasn't enough but a small penlight torch provided a narrow, bright beam that wouldn't be obvious from outside.

Fliss shone it briefly on Maria's face. Tear-streaked and terrified, the young mother was far paler than normal, and when Fliss touched her skin, it was cool and clammy.

'It's going to be all right, Maria,' Fliss said with a conviction she was far from feeling herself. 'We're going to get through this.'

'But what's happening? And why are you dressed like that?'

Fliss pulled the black hat from her head. 'Sorry. I must look a bit weird. Jack thought I'd be obvious if I didn't cover up.'

'Cover up from what? What's going on? Who's got a gun and *why* are they shooting at us?'

'They?' Seth's question was a demand for more information. 'You saw more than one person?'

'Yes.'

'How many?'

'I... I'm not sure. It was so dark. I was running... and then I fell... and then it started to hurt and...'

'It's okay, love.' Fliss shot Seth a warning glance. Her patient was distressed enough without being interrogated. Seth nodded curtly and began talking quietly and rapidly into his microphone.

Fliss looked up at Angus as she reached for a blood-pressure cuff. 'Do you know what's going on?'

He was uncovering the wound on Maria's leg and held out a hand for the torch.

'I'm not up with the latest info. My radio transmissions are a bit patchy. I think something got damaged when I tackled you. What I do know is that it appears some locals have got caught up with a drugs ring. We think this started because someone was being warned off and it's escalated. Whoever's involved isn't too bothered if innocent people get in the way.'

'Are you talking about cannabis?' Maria gave a short, unamused huff of laughter. 'They're trying to kill people for the sake of a bit of hooch?'

'Not "a bit",' Seth put in. 'We're probably talking about major production here. The kind of multi-million-dollar operation that requires large areas of plantation.'

'And it could be that a cannabis operation is just part of something bigger,' Angus added. 'Like methamphetamine production. Easy to hide a lab in the kind of bush around here. It could be that someone knows more than they should.' He glanced up. 'The bleeding's stopped, Fliss. I need to get a dressing on this again, and have you got a traction splint available?'

'Yes. There's one in the storeroom.' Fliss let down the pressure in the cuff. 'Blood pressure's ninety-five on fifty. I'm going to start some fluids.' She eyed the cannula taped to Maria's forearm. 'What gauge did you use?'

'Sixteen,' Angus responded. 'I knew she'd need fluids as well as the pain relief.'

'You gave her morphine?'

'Yes. Five milligrams.'

'And an anti-emetic?'

'Yes.'

'How's the pain at the moment, Maria?'

'It still hurts.'

'We'll give you some more morphine in a minute, before we splint your leg.'

'This... isn't going to hurt the baby, is it?'

'No,' Fliss said reassuringly. 'We're going to take the best care of you, and that way we'll be looking after baby as well.'

She went to the storeroom with only the light from the tiny torch to locate the traction splint and a bag of saline. As she attached the giving set to the cannula and hung the bag of fluids, Fliss found herself thinking about what Angus and Seth had been saying about the quiet little township of Morriston being possibly caught up in a major drugs bust. Had she really thought that by coming here she would be immune to the kinds of problems she had encountered all too often in a big city emergency department? Had that, in fact, blinded her to something she could have spotted earlier?

'I had a patient a couple of weeks ago,' she told Angus. 'He wanted something for his eczema. His arms were scratched to bits.'

Angus was on her wavelength instantly. 'Did you notice anything else?'

'He talked fast. Kind of mumbled.'

'You think he might be a methamphetamine user?'

'It's possible, in hindsight. I thought he was a bit odd but then I thought I was being biased. I knew he killed and stuffed possums for a living, which I thought was really gross.'

'Darren?' Maria's eyes widened. 'You think Darren shot me? No way! I've known him since he was a kid. We went to school together.'

'Do you know if he uses drugs?'

'He's always smoked a lot. He used to get into trouble at school for it. I haven't really had anything to do with him for years, though. I did hear he'd been in trouble with the police a while back. For burglary, I think.'

Angus raised an eyebrow. 'Maybe possums aren't enough to support a serious habit.'

'If he's using something like P, it could have changed his personality from what you remember, Maria,' Fliss said. 'People can get paranoid. Violent. It could explain what's happening out there.' She looked up at Angus. 'Couldn't it?'

The acknowledgment was a brief nod. 'You want to top up that morphine? I'd like to get this splint on.'

The extra pain relief was clearly welcome. Fliss had to raise Maria's leg while Angus slipped the splint underneath and attached the figure-of-eight strap to hold the foot of the broken limb. Then the tension was wound on until the leg was the same length as her unbroken one. Fliss pulled the wide Velcro straps into place at intervals up the leg, avoiding the dressing over the open gunshot wound.

'You're going to need surgery to clean this up and repair the bone damage,' Fliss warned their patient. 'We'll get you to a hospital as soon as we can.'

'When will that be?'

There was a moment's awkward silence.

'When it's safe,' Angus said.

Maria's eyes filled with tears. 'I want to go home. Ben will be getting worried by now.' She caught Fliss's arm. 'What if he gets the truck out and comes looking for me? And brings the girls?'

The anxiety was contagious. There was no phone at Maria's isolated farmlet. No way of reassuring her family or warning them not to come into the village.

'The roads are all covered,' Angus said. 'There's no way they'll get anywhere close enough to be in danger. I'll try and get a message through but I can't promise anything.'

Fliss had to look away. She fiddled with the little blue wheel on the IV line, making an unnecessary adjustment to what was already the fastest flow rate.

Of course Angus couldn't promise anything. That had always been the problem, hadn't it?

He hadn't been able to promise he wouldn't get called away on any of those first dates they'd had, over a year ago now. The pager he had with him twenty-four hours of every day could go off at any time.

He could never promise to be home at a certain time or to complete the chores he had willingly taken responsibility for when they had started to live together only weeks after their first date.

And he certainly couldn't have promised not to take risks in his job. Risks that could well mean he would never come home at all.

At least he was honest enough not to make promises when the keeping of them was out of his control. Echoes of the deep, rumbly voice of her father, which always seemed to be on the brink of laughter, sounded in a far corner of her mind.

'*Be back in the morning, button – I promise.*'

Or '*See you tonight, sweets – I promise.*'

And for her mother, '*Don't worry so much, darling. I'll be back –
I promise.*'

As a child, Fliss had never been able to understand why those
promises hadn't given her mother the same comfort they had
given her.

The woman she was now could understand the anxiety in
Maria's face, but there were no promises Fliss could make either.
She could only offer the comfort her skills could reliably provide
as she made a thorough check on both Maria and the baby.

The sound of the strong, steady foetal heartbeat they all
heard a few minutes later made them smile.

But Fliss made the mistake of catching Angus's glance as she
smiled – sharing the hope they all felt in that moment that
somehow everything was going to be all right.

It had been a very similar moment that had started everything
between Angus and Fliss, on a day when Angus and his partner
had brought in a patient with serious chest trauma. Fliss had
been given a leading role in the drama of opening the man's chest
in the emergency department – a desperate and usually futile
attempt to save a life. On that occasion, however, it had been
successful and the bleeding from a ruptured major vessel had
been controlled well enough for the young man to make it as far
as Theatre.

Angus had been there. Unwilling to give up on a patient he
had already struggled to stabilise. Ready to assist the new senior
registrar who had landed such a major case on one of her first
shifts. Openly admiring of her skills.

Of *her*.

And that shared glance, when it had become apparent they
had succeeded, had been enough to spark so much more.

Something was still smouldering despite everything that had
happened since. Fliss could tell because she could feel it burning.

Tendrils of flame that ignited somewhere deep in her abdomen and spread instantaneously. The hint of remembered passion was more than enough to bring the pain of its ending way too close to the surface.

It still hurt.

The smile prompted by the healthy sound of Maria's baby's heartbeat vanished. Fliss removed the foetal stethoscope and pulled back the blanket to cover Maria. If only it could be that easy to pull a cover over the raw patch on her soul.

How many more reminders would there be before this was all over?

Fliss needed a distraction. She would take another complete set of vital-sign measurements on Maria, she decided, picking up the bulb of the blood-pressure cuff in preparation for inflating it.

'Stop!'

The command from Seth, still standing close to the window, was quiet but stern enough for Fliss to freeze.

To hold her breath.

They all froze. The silence was absolute for just a split second.

Then they all heard it.

A soft, scratching sound coming from outside. Someone was moving in the shrubbery beneath the window.

Someone who was trying to avoid detection.

4

'Put that *away*!'

Fliss was appalled at the speed with which Seth had drawn a revolver from its holster and primed it for action.

'You're *not* going to shoot someone in my surgery.'

'He's trying to protect you,' Angus snapped. 'There's someone outside. Get down on the floor, Fliss.'

Maria couldn't very well cower on the floor, could she, with her whole leg in a splint and an IV line tying her to the bed? Fliss felt her patient reaching out for her hand in fear, and she grabbed it back and squeezed. Hard.

'I'm not going anywhere,' she announced.

'Shh!' Seth had his back to the wall but was inching sideways, presumably to peer through the gap left at the edge of the window by the ill-fitting curtains.

The rattle at the door of the surgery sounded far too loud a second later in the tense silence. Fliss jumped. Maria gasped in horror.

'*Fliss!*'

The croaky call was a kind of whispered shout. Impossible to identify.

'You in there, lass?'

'It's *Jack*,' Fliss said in relief. 'Let him in – quickly!'

But neither of the men moved. Judging by the way Angus tilted his head and then touched the spot where the balaclava covered an earpiece, they were both listening to a message coming through their communication system.

'Roger,' Seth said quietly. 'Anything else on the move?'

'*Fliss!*'

The call was louder. More urgent.

'Oh, for heaven's sake!' Fliss let go of Maria's hand and marched into the waiting area. She had unlocked the door and was about to pull it open when Angus grabbed her arm and hauled her to one side.

'But it's *Jack*,' she protested.

'Are you sure about that?'

'Of course I'm sure. He's the only person around here that ever calls me "lass".'

Silence again. Just for a heartbeat. And then another. Jack might be the only person in this vicinity who used the Scottish term as an endearment, but it had been as much a part of Angus McBride's vocabulary as his soft accent.

A softly spoken word that had slipped out more than once, usually in conjunction with whispered words of love to cloak her heart when she'd lain in his arms at night in those early, blissful days of their love affair.

Too long ago.

Far enough away in time and place to have been on a different planet. It shouldn't be enough to fuel those smouldering embers, but it was. Fliss had to break eye contact with Angus. Had to look away before she revealed something she didn't even want to admit to herself.

'Right.' A terse word that dismissed anything remotely personal.

Angus opened the door so swiftly that Jack almost fell into the waiting room. He wasn't very well balanced in any case, because he had his single arm around the waist of a small boy whose arms were wrapped around the old man's neck.

'You found him.' Fliss reached out, barely aware of Angus shutting and relocking the door. 'Is it Cody? Is he all right?'

'Callum.' Jack relinquished his burden and then bent forward, supporting himself with his hand on a knee as he struggled for breath. 'Hurt... Must have been... first... to get shot.'

The six-year-old boy whimpered. 'My tummy hurts,' he told Fliss.

It was hard to know what to do first. Jack looked terrible, gasping for air and barely able to stay upright, but Fliss had her arms full with a child who was in pain and potentially badly injured.

'I'll take the boy.' Strong arms lifted Callum from her own. 'You bring Jack in.'

The consulting room was suddenly far too small. With a sweep of his arm, Angus cleared Fliss's desk and laid Callum on the hard wooden surface.

'Sit down here, Jack,' Fliss told the old man. 'Against the wall. I'll get a pillow to help you sit forward a bit.'

He needed oxygen urgently. Far more than the token amount Maria was receiving through the nasal cannula.

'I'm going to take this off for a minute,' Fliss warned her first patient. 'Jack needs oxygen more than you do at the moment but I've got another cylinder in the storeroom when we get sorted.'

'Go for it,' Maria urged. She cast an anxious glance at the new patients in the surgery. 'I'm fine.'

Fliss attached a high concentration mask to the cylinder and slipped the elastic band over Jack's head.

'Don't try to talk,' she warned him. 'Let's get your breathing sorted first.'

Jack nodded. He looked as though he was trying to smile beneath the mask, but the effort was half-hearted. He looked exhausted. His eyes were half-shut and what little skin she could see between smears of boot polish looked grey. How hard must it have been for him to carry a child? With the episode of worsening heart failure Jack had at present, it could have been enough to kill him. It still could.

But he had found Callum. And brought him to Fliss for treatment. It was only now that he was allowing his body to register the toll taken. Fliss found herself squeezing another hand.

'You did it, Jack. I'm so proud of you.'

Fliss could feel the glance that flashed in her direction from where Angus was making a preliminary examination of Callum. A raised eyebrow sort of glance, as though he was surprised – or disapproving, perhaps, of the bond Fliss might have with a rather disreputable-looking patient. The glance barely registered, however. They both had far too much else to think about.

The return squeeze of her hand that Fliss received from Jack was encouraging, but there was no time to register pleasure either. Fliss felt as though she had stepped into an entire emergency department full of patients urgently needing her care. Her brain focused sharply but she could feel compartments forming. It was possible to do more than one thing at once and still do it well when you had these kinds of adrenaline levels flowing.

Jack needed the lifepack electrodes on so she could see a trace of his heart rhythm. He needed an IV line and a hefty dose of diuretic on board. If his breathing became any more laboured he would require help with a ventilator mask, and if his blood pressure was still at an acceptably high level, Fliss would add nitrates to the drugs she would use to combat the heart failure. Some morphine might help as well but the risk of respiratory arrest had to be taken into account. Covering bases in case there was an underlying cardiac event causing the failure also had to be considered. Aspirin. Anticoagulation. Subcutaneous heparin, possibly?

A plan of action for Jack formed as Fliss listened to his chest with her stethoscope, but her gaze was on the man bending over the child on her desk.

'How's Callum looking, Gus?' Fliss didn't even notice she had used the shortened form of his name that only people close to him were invited to use.

'Abdominal wound. Looks like a gunshot. I can't see any exit wound so I'm assuming the bullet's still in there somewhere.'

Callum whimpered loudly.

'Sorry, buddy,' Angus said quietly. 'I know it hurts, mate.'

Fliss knew that the paramedic's touch would be as gentle as his words. She had seen him work with children. She had once thought what an amazing father he would make. But she couldn't afford to give mental energy to anything more than a fleeting gratitude that he was here to help right now. And that he would be the best person to help look after a sad and frightened small boy.

'Blood pressure?' she queried briskly.

'Haven't taken it yet. Radial pulse is present but weak. He's tachycardic.'

He would be bleeding internally. The only unknown was how bad that bleeding was. Having a radial pulse still present wasn't as reassuring in a child as it would have been in an adult. Children could compensate well with even massive blood loss for some time. Then they could crash. Catastrophically.

'Can you get some fluids started, please?'

'I'm just looking for a vein,' Angus responded. 'I'd like to get some morphine on board as well.'

'There's IV gear in that first drawer of the cabinet beside the bed and there's more in the storeroom. First shelf on the right as you go in. Could you bring me an eighteen-gauge cannula and a tourniquet, too, please?'

'Sure.'

'And I'll need an alcohol wipe and a saline flush.'

'Of course.'

Fliss felt her tension ease just a fraction. She hadn't needed to tell Angus what else she needed. He knew. In stabilising a critically injured patient in an environment away from an emergency department, he was just as qualified as she was. And a lot more experienced. Her relief at having him working by her side increased several notches.

She moved to lift the lifepack from its shelf beside the examination table, sparing just a second to check on Maria.

'How are you feeling?'

'Not so bad. The morphine's helped a lot. My leg doesn't hurt much at all at the moment.'

'Good. Anything else bothering you?'

Stupid question. Maria's wry smile acknowledged the enormity of what was bothering them all. It also let Fliss know that her energies needed to be directed towards what was happening within the walls of their haven rather than the unknown danger outside.

The lifepack was set on the floor beside Jack, and Fliss swiftly attached the electrodes. The rhythm that appeared on the small screen wasn't comforting. Jack's heart was struggling to provide enough oxygen to keep itself functioning well, let alone the rest of his body.

Angus dropped a handful of IV gear beside her on his way back to the desk, and for several minutes they worked separately on their patients, concentrating on finding venous access and getting fluids and medications started.

'Keep really still for me, mate,' Angus encouraged Callum. 'You'll feel a wee scratch on your arm.'

'Okay, Jack. I'm going to give you some medication now,' Fliss said. 'We're going to get on top of this soon, I promise.'

It wasn't an empty promise. At least it wouldn't be if there was anything humanly possible Fliss could do. And even if it was, Jack needed the reassurance. It was as much a part of the treatment as anything else.

Angus and Fliss got each other to check the drugs they'd administered. Diuretics and nitrates for Jack, pain relief and anti-nausea for Callum.

'We need something more comfortable to put Callum on,' Angus said eventually.

Fliss nodded. She wanted to make Jack more comfortable as well. There was no question of moving Maria from the bed, and they had no idea how long it would be until they could evacuate their patients. Or whether they would end up with more people to treat before this was over. Innovation was called for.

'We could get rid of the chairs from the waiting room,' Fliss suggested. 'And get the mattress and pillows from my bed in the cottage. There's all the squabs and cushions from the couch and armchairs as well.'

'What do you reckon, Seth?' Angus looked to his colleague for a second opinion.

'You don't need to go outside?'

'Not if we can unlock the interior door from this side,' Fliss told him. 'I think there's a spare key in my desk drawer.'

'You find the key. I'll check with the boss and then make sure the house is safe to enter if we get the go-ahead.'

The sound of the desk drawer opening made Callum open his drowsy eyes. 'Dr Fliss?'

'Hi, sweetheart. How's that tummy feeling now?'

'Better.' But the child's eyes filled with tears. 'Why did Darren shoot me?'

'It was Darren that shot you?' Although the suspicion had been there, it was shocking to think that someone who was a part of this small community could have done such a thing.

Seth had stopped his quiet words into the microphone attached to his collar. He was listening intently to Callum, who nodded solemnly.

A fat tear rolled down his cheek. 'He said we were spying on him and that we were going to tell, but we weren't. We were just riding our bikes.'

We.

Fliss brushed the tear away. 'I know, darling.' She tried to keep her voice steady. 'Where's Cody, do you know? Was... was he hurt, too?'

'I don't know.' More tears flowed. 'He started crying and ran away.' A sob made him choke on the last words. 'I want him back. And I want Mum.'

'I know.' Fliss stroked his forehead and bent to drop a kiss onto damp skin beneath blond curls. The twins were identical. And inseparable. Fliss had never seen one of the boys alone before. 'But don't worry. We're going to take care of you until we find everyone else.'

She turned to Seth. 'Can you let someone know that there's another six-year-old boy out there? He needs to be found.'

Seth nodded.

'Any word on how soon we're going to be able to evacuate patients?'

'Negative. Risk of moving anybody is too high at present.'

'I don't like him.' Callum seemed to be pointing at both Angus and Seth. 'He's got a gun.'

'Only so he can look after us, buddy.' Angus stepped closer. 'But *I* haven't got a gun. Honest.'

Fliss fished the key out from beneath a layer of paperclips and ballpoint pens in the drawer as Callum responded to Angus and stopped crying. The soothing words continued and as Fliss handed the key to Seth, she could see that the boy was almost asleep. The fact he was happier was good but not reassuring.

Callum needed urgent investigations. A CT scan. A laparotomy. It would be wishful thinking to hope that he had a bullet in his abdomen that had miraculously missed doing any damage to major vessels or vital organs. If an artery had been clipped or his spleen or liver damaged, the child could bleed to death and there would be nothing Fliss could do to prevent it. Her surgery was not equipped for anything other than minor procedures, and Fliss was not a surgeon.

For the first time since she had fled the city, Fliss longed to be back in the brightly lit and often chaotic environment of a large emergency department. One with back-up available. Experts in any field she could need. Equipment and technology. Operating theatres and intensive care. Angus had the advantage over her here. At least he was used to working away from a hospital. Relying on the equipment and skills he had readily available. Fliss was going to need him to help her through this.

It was possible that Angus would need *her* support as well. He might look as though he was used to dealing with this kind of situation, but Fliss knew that paramedic protocols called for evacuation to the nearest hospital at the earliest possible opportunity for seriously injured patients, and right now that wasn't on the agenda.

When Seth had checked the inside of the cottage, Fliss quickly moved several chairs and replaced them with squabs and cushions. She grabbed some towels and sheets from the meagre contents of her linen cupboard. The two sofa squabs made a bed just the right size for a small child. Angus gently lifted the sleepy boy and placed him on the makeshift bed.

'I'll need some help with the mattress,' Fliss said. 'Seth?'

'I need to keep watch on the street.'

'Angus?'

'Sure. Let's go.'

'Wait.' Fliss was reluctant to leave the surgery with no medic in attendance even if it was only going to be for a minute or two. 'I just want to check on everybody again first.'

It was like a rapid-fire mini ward round, with a quick set of vital-sign measurements and an assessment of the current condition on all their charges. They were all drowsy. Maria's pain medication was still effective and her blood pressure had risen slightly, which was good. Jack was exhausted, but the probe on his finger that allowed the lifepack to record the level of oxygen saturation in his blood revealed a significant improvement. His heart rate had slowed to a more normal level as well.

'We're going to get a mattress, Jack, and make you a lot more comfortable.'

'No need.' Jack's voice was muffled by a mask that looked full of boot-polish-stained beard. 'I'm fine.'

'You will be,' Fliss agreed. 'But only if you do what you're told.'

The next word from her patient was clear enough to elicit a quick grin from Angus.

'Bossy!'

Callum was asleep but roused when Fliss pressed her hand gently to his belly.

'*Ow-w.*'

'Sorry, love. I just need to check what's going on.' She caught Angus's gaze. 'Abdo's still soft. Pain's more upper right quadrant, which is well away from the entry wound.'

He nodded. 'Spleen, you reckon?'

'Quite possibly.' Fliss slipped a hand beneath Callum and he moaned again. 'I think there's rib involvement, too.' She pulled her stethoscope from around her neck. 'Chest's clear,' she announced a short time later. 'Equal air entry but remind me to keep a close watch on it, will you?'

'Sure.' Angus deflated the blood-pressure cuff. 'Seventy-eight on fifty.'

'No change, then.' It was still just sitting on the lowest end of a normal range for a child his age. Fliss chewed the inside of her lip for a second. They were all stable. For now. She looked at Seth. 'Can you watch him, please? And the others? Yell if anything at all changes.'

Seth gave a single nod. 'Don't turn on any lights. Just take the torch like you did last time.'

The interior door of the surgery opened into a laundry area with a washing machine and dryer. That led into the kitchen and then the narrow central hallway from which four doors opened. Two bedrooms, one of which was used as an office, a sitting room and a bathroom.

The irony of leading Angus directly to her bedroom was not lost on Fliss. He would have to be the last person she had expected in this house, let alone a room that could only remind them both of how close they had once been.

It didn't help that the light from the tiny torch flickered as she entered her bedroom. Her forward movement faltered long enough for Angus to bump into her from behind.

'Sorry.'

He had caught her arms to prevent her from stumbling. Fliss could feel the strength in his hands. Could feel how close he was as he pulled her back so she could regain her balance.

Fliss could feel the barrier of the bullet-proof vest he wore. A solid wall between their bodies. It should have been enough to remind her of why things hadn't worked and could never work.

But it wasn't.

For a moment Fliss had to fight the urge to turn. To put her arms around his neck and have Angus hold her close. To feel that ultimate bliss of loving... and being loved.

To raise her face and invite the touch of his lips and a kiss that Fliss knew she could lose herself in. Instantly and utterly.

But the beam of light from the tiny torch was strong again.

As Fliss needed to be.

It was totally inappropriate to allow anything personal to interfere with what needed to be done. Not only unprofessional – it would be a huge backward step in the recovery process Fliss had embarked on by coming here in the first place.

'Lucky it's only a single mattress,' she said briskly. Then she kicked herself mentally. Why on earth had she said that? Would Angus take it as she'd meant it – that it would be much less of a hassle to move into the surgery? Or would he realise that her thoughts had been distracted by something far more personal and think that she was trying to drive away memories that could surface in sharing the task of moving a larger mattress?

Angus didn't appear to be aware of her lapse.

'We'll just take the mattress and pillows, shall we? We can always duck back if we need more blankets or something.'

'Okay.' Fliss pulled the duvet clear of the bed and Angus lifted the narrow, inner-sprung mattress from the base of the bed with ease. It appeared that Fliss would only be needed to carry the pillows, but then the mattress got caught as Angus tried to turn it into the narrow hallway.

'Back up a bit,' he instructed Fliss. 'I'll stand it on its end.'

They got as far as the kitchen and then Fliss needed to push the small table and dining chairs out of the way.

'Maybe I can get back here in a bit and make us all a hot drink or something.'

'Sounds good.'

'I wish I'd been to the supermarket today.' Fliss eyed her fridge, wondering how much milk she had available. 'I wasn't expecting to be trying to run my own hospital under siege conditions.'

Angus snorted. 'You're enjoying this, aren't you, Fliss?'

'*What?*'

The suggestion was shocking. Or was this simply retaliation for the same accusation she had levelled at Angus back in the cemetery? If so, Fliss was quite prepared to bite back.

'Are you kidding? I'm scared stiff. And I'm seriously worried about how I'm going to cope with keeping these people stable until we can get them to a hospital.'

'You don't look scared stiff,' Angus informed her. 'You're coping with multiple patients and now you're planning ahead.'

'I... Ah...' Of course she was planning ahead. Thinking of what her patients and their carers might need in the next few hours. There was satisfaction to be found in coping with what was an unimaginable turn of events, but *enjoying* it? You'd have to be sick to get a buzz out of something like this.

Like Angus was? Was this what had driven him into, and keeping him in, a career like this?

'I'm *not* enjoying this.' Fliss picked up one end of the mattress with her free hand, pointing the small torch with the other to illuminate the awkward path they had to take past the washing machine and dryer. She tugged hard. They were wasting time and she needed to get back to her patients. 'I loathe violence. You *know* that.'

Angus seemed to be a dead weight in the darkness, anchoring the other end of the mattress. 'Hang on a tick. I need to talk to you, Fliss.'

'What about?'

'Do you remember the first time we met?'

This was hardly the time or place for a trip down memory lane, but she did remember, didn't she? She'd been thinking of it only a matter of minutes ago, in fact. 'What's that got to do with anything?'

'You were cracking someone's chest.'

'So?'

The mattress hadn't moved. Fliss tugged again ineffectually. Angus seemed to think that their conversation was important enough to waste time, but would Seth actually recognise a deterioration in any of the injured or sick people he was watching fast enough to summon them in time if Jack or Callum crashed?

They'd only been absent for a minute, though. Maybe two. And they were only a few steps away now. The temptation to continue talking to Angus was undeniable. There was something about his tone. The stillness of the huge, dark figure only a few feet away. Maybe it was important enough to sacrifice a little more time.

'It's a pretty violent thing to do, don't you think?' Angus said. 'Ripping open someone's chest? Under most circumstances it would be more than enough to kill them.'

Fliss could feel her jaw dropping. Was Angus suggesting she was *attracted* to violence?

'I was trying to save someone's life,' she snapped. 'And it worked, remember?'

'Oh, I remember,' Angus said quietly. 'And I remember how happy you were at the end of the case.'

'Of course I was happy. It was a great case. He survived.' Fliss let out a breath in an indignant huff. 'It doesn't mean I go around hoping people are going to get dangerously ill or suffer violent trauma so that I can get some job satisfaction.'

Like she'd once accused Angus of doing. Fliss pulled really hard on the mattress and this time it moved. She dragged it into the laundry.

'I do the opposite, actually,' she told Angus. 'I see what I do as making a statement against violence. Intervening in the hope of helping people to avoid some of the repercussions.'

'Funny,' Angus murmured. 'That's pretty much how I see *my* job.'

The end of the mattress caught on the edge of the washing machine and Fliss lost her one-handed grip. She turned and used her foot to try and shift the mattress. Angus had been back in her life for such a short time. How on earth had they managed to start arguing about their differing philosophies again so easily? Nothing had changed, had it? Fliss should just ignore the jibe but she couldn't. It was touching a fresh scar that the reappearance of this man had just scratched open.

'I don't risk my life to intervene,' she said crisply. 'Not under normal circumstances, anyway.'

'Don't you?' Angus dropped his end of the mattress and squeezed along the wall to lift the other end clear of the washing machine. 'What about the risk of hepatitis or HIV or some nasty virus like SARS or Covid or a new type of flu?'

Fliss was silent. Those risks came with the territory. You took precautions to reduce the risk but to some degree it was unavoidable and therefore had to be accepted.

Was it so unreasonable to accept that Angus felt the same way about his job?

'And what about violent patients?' Angus moved away again. 'There's been more than one staff member attacked by someone who's psychotic.'

'We have security.'

The silence from the other end of the mattress was eloquent. Angus had better security than anyone in an emergency department could hope for. Highly trained and armed police officers at his side the whole time. They could only call security in a hospital environment after the risk became evident.

They were moving again. Any second now and they would be back in the waiting area of the surgery. In company. Well away from any opportunity to revisit personal territory, which was just as well because Fliss felt confused.

Maybe what they did wasn't so different after all. Maybe it was just a matter of the degree to which they became involved.

Fliss wouldn't do what Angus did for anything. If she'd had any choice she would be a million miles away from the situation they were currently in.

Someone would always be there, though. Some innocent person caught up in it. Like Maria. And poor little Callum. What if people like Angus and his colleagues didn't respond to calls like this and rush out to help them?

How would Fliss feel if she was here alone and terrified?

Maybe she couldn't have faced living with a man who made a career out of this sort of thing, but right now Fliss suddenly felt inordinately proud of Angus and what he did for a living, and that was as confusing as the thought that they aimed for the same kind of satisfaction from their chosen work.

The pride was fierce enough to bring the sting of tears to her eyes, and Fliss was grateful it was far too dark for Angus to notice. She stood back, having dragged her end of the mattress through the doorway into the waiting area, allowing Angus to push it the rest of the way. As he came through the doorway, he paused and for just a moment Fliss could see his face clearly in the edge of the beam her torch emitted. He would be able to see hers as well, she realised, and she quickly blinked to clear any excess moisture from her eyes.

Fliss even managed to smile.

'Hey,' she said softly.

Angus raised an eyebrow. 'What?'

What, indeed? Words rushed to the tip of her tongue. Fliss was so close to confessing how badly she had missed having Angus in her life in the last few months. How much she missed hearing his voice. Feeling the touch of his hands... and lips. Just *being* with him. The words tangled together as they reached the warning sign flashing from the back of her mind.

'I'm just... glad you're here,' Fliss whispered.

He didn't smile but there was a softening around his eyes, as though any tension from their recent conversation had evaporated.

'So am I,' he whispered back. 'And try not to worry too much. We'll get through this.'

Fliss nodded and bit her lip to stop it wobbling. 'Yeah. We will. We're working on the same side, aren't we?'

A quick smile now. A wry one.

'We always were,' Angus murmured. 'You just couldn't see it.'

5

The flash of pride came from nowhere and its strength was disconcerting.

Angus had no right to feel proud of Fliss any longer, did he? Pride in someone else for who they were or what they did implied a bond. You could feel proud of a colleague, or a family member, or a friend, and especially of a partner, but Fliss fitted into none of those categories now.

Worse luck.

Dr Felicity Slade now seemed to have a closer bond with the inhabitants of this small west-coast township than she had with him, judging by the reaction she got from Jack after being away from the surgery for only a few minutes.

The old man's eyes fairly lit up. He still looked as sick as a dog, though, and Fliss spent some time recording all his vital signs, running off a new ECG, adjusting his medication and listening to his chest before they moved him to the mattress Angus had positioned in the waiting area, at right angles to the cushion bed that Callum was occupying.

Callum was roused from his drowsiness by the activity close

at hand and began crying for his brother. Angus bent over the small boy.

'It's okay, buddy,' he said soothingly.

'No... no...' Callum sobbed. 'I want Dr Fliss.'

Fliss stroked the child's hair and spoke reassuringly, but Callum reached up and wound his arms around her neck, and she ended up cuddling her small patient properly. She looked over his head at Angus.

'His fluids have almost run through. Could you grab another bag of saline from the storeroom, please?'

'Sure.'

The continuing sound of gunfire, although distant, made Angus stop by the examination couch in the surgery on his way to the storeroom.

'You okay, Maria?'

'I'm scared.'

'I know.' Angus glanced at Seth, who was still stationed near the window. 'Who's firing out there? Our guys or them?'

Seth shrugged. 'Haven't heard anything so I assume it's them.'

Angus gave Maria what he hoped was a reassuring smile. 'Sounds like they're getting further away from us, at any rate. How's the leg feeling?'

'Not too bad, I guess.'

Angus could see that tears were imminent. He could also see that Maria was looking past him to where the low, comforting murmur of Fliss's voice was coming from. 'Would you like to talk to Fliss?'

Maria caught her bottom lip with her teeth. Her nod was embarrassed. 'Only when she's not so busy with the others,' she said apologetically. Her smile acknowledged that Angus was doing his best. 'It's just that she's... a friend, you know? She's great to talk to.'

Angus had no trouble nodding agreement. He'd always found Fliss great to talk to. At the beginning, anyway. And he knew perfectly well the kind of comfort she was capable of imparting. He'd talked to her for an entire night once – about a week after they had decided they wanted to live together. Only a month or so after their first date, but they had both been so much in love and it had happened so naturally.

Losing a young patient that day had been the first dampener on the joy of being together for so much more of their time. It had been gutting. A tractor roll-over accident way up in the high country, and by the time the helicopter had made it to the scene, the crush injuries the toddler had sustained had been too severe to stabilise. Angus had done his utmost, but the boy had died just as they were landing on the hospital helipad.

Talking it through with Fliss and examining everything he'd done and what else could have been possible and what simply hadn't been possible had, to some degree, absolved him from guilt. The only way to assuage the pain of having lost such a young patient had been far more personal, however. Through eye contact and touch and just being with someone who loved him. They hadn't made love that night – there was no way Angus would have wanted to – but lying beside Fliss and being held in her arms had been exactly what he'd needed.

He'd never felt so close to another human being in his life.

Had never loved anyone that much.

Could never love anyone else that much.

He could hear that gentle tone in her voice a few minutes later, when Fliss took the time to reassure Maria. He had seen the flash of fear in Fliss's eyes at the sound of much closer gunfire than the last round, but she carried on with a resolution that amazed Angus.

Instinctively, her caring nature let her say and do exactly the right thing – as she had done with him that night. Assuring Maria of her own and her family's current safety thanks to the presence of the team that included Angus, Fliss led Maria into feeling hopeful about the future.

'I saw Grace talking to Mrs McKay in the shop the other day.' Angus could hear the smile in Fliss's voice. 'She's growing up so fast!'

'She's only just turned seven,' Maria responded proudly, 'but I don't know how I'd manage without her to help me with all the young ones.'

'It sounded as though she was looking for things for Christmas. She was asking where to find silver foil and tinsel and all sorts of stuff like that.'

Maria actually chuckled. 'She's on a mission to make decorations. We've got a fir tree growing in the middle of our lawn and that's our Christmas tree. It must be twenty feet high now but Ben still climbs all the way to the top to put the star on.'

'Do you put the presents outside as well?'

'They get hidden all around the garden. It's like a big treasure hunt and it usually lasts until we have our dinner, but I'm not sure about this year. Grace and Ruby are getting too clever about finding things. It might be all over by breakfast-time.'

'Sounds fun. Christmas must be magic with so many children around. And this year you'll have a brand-new baby – it'll be even more special.'

The tone made Angus turn his head sharply, and he could feel a frown crease his forehead. She sounded... wistful. But hadn't she told him she didn't want children?

A seed of hope blossomed somewhere deep. Maybe Fliss had changed her mind after getting to know a family like Maria's. Maybe it could even provide a starting point to finding their way back to each other. Angus wanted children.

He wanted Fliss to be the mother of those children.

So much for having moved on. He'd tried so hard to get over Fliss, too. To put his life back together after she'd shattered it by moving out. Even now, his head was issuing warnings tinged with real alarm.

Don't go there!

You know what it was like when she left!

You'll just get hurt all over again! It could never work!

You're incompatible!

If they were so incompatible, why did they both look up at precisely the same moment, catch each other's gaze and then both look towards where Callum was lying?

The sound the child had made was worrying, that was why.

It had started as a whimper but turned into a quiet but odd sort of gasp.

Fliss was there in seconds. She didn't even duck her head at the crack of gunfire that was close enough to make Seth raise his own weapon and flatten himself against the wall to peer outside again. He spoke tersely into his microphone, reporting the development and requesting an update of information. Fliss didn't seem aware of the escalating tension. She was completely focused on her youngest patient.

'What is it, sweetheart? Are you having trouble breathing?'

Callum didn't respond. His breathing was obviously too laboured to allow for speech. What was even more worrying was that he didn't open his eyes properly. His head rolled to one side as Fliss laid her stethoscope on the small chest, and as Angus shone the torch he was holding on the boy's face, he could see the bluish tinge to Callum's lips.

'Breath sounds absent on the right side,' Fliss reported, sounding grim. 'I think I was right about that rib injury.'

Angus had been moving the torch with one hand while he felt

for Callum's pulse with the other. 'Neck veins are distended and I can't find a radial pulse.'

They both knew what was happening here but clear communication was still paramount. The injury to Callum's ribs must have been enough to damage deeper tissues. Air was escaping into the chest cavity outside his lungs and enough was accumulating to compromise his breathing. It was a potentially fatal complication.

'Pneumothorax?'

'Tensioning,' Fliss agreed. 'And I don't have a chest drain kit.' Frustration made her sound angry.

'I've got a decompression needle in my kit.' Angus moved fast. 'Seth, could you grab the other oxygen cylinder from the storeroom? It's the black one with a white top. Try and find a small-sized mask, too.'

'What's happening?' Jack pulled the mask from his face as Angus dropped his kit and ripped open the zip fastenings. 'Give the lad this one, Fliss. I don't need it any more.'

'Yes, you do,' Fliss said, 'but I'll use it until we get the other cylinder.' She took the oversized adult mask from Jack and slipped the elastic band over Callum's head.

'We'll fix this, sweetheart,' she murmured. 'You just hang in there.'

'He's not going to die, is he?' Jack sounded hoarse and he struggled to move. 'Can I help?'

'You can help by staying right where you are, Jack,' Fliss said firmly. 'And try not to worry. Callum's in a spot of trouble right now with his breathing but we can deal with this.'

Angus was ripping open packages. 'I've got a fourteen-gauge cannula, a three-way stopcock and a fifty-mil syringe.'

'It'll be a good start, anyway.'

Angus picked up an alcohol wipe and the torch. He held the

wipe out to Fliss, but she didn't move. 'I thought you were going to do this,' she said.

Angus was astonished. Fliss was the more highly qualified medical professional present. 'Do you want me to?'

Fliss nodded swiftly. 'You've got the advantage in experience. I'm more au fait with inserting tubes and connecting them to underwater seal drains.'

'Fine.' Angus didn't want to waste even another second. He swabbed at the area on Callum's chest just under his collarbone, where the needle needed to be inserted. Second intercostal space, midclavicular line. As the needle touched the skin, Angus was pleased to notice that his hand was rock steady.

He wanted to do this perfectly. Fliss trusted him. He would do anything she asked him to, he thought fleetingly, and he would always do it to the utmost best of his ability.

No. The faint cry from somewhere in his head was there for only a heartbeat. *Not true*, it prodded. *You weren't prepared to change your career, were you?*

That was different. Such a ridiculous rebuttal that Angus found it easy to squash it into oblivion and concentrate totally on the job at hand. The job that Fliss had asked him to do.

Callum's level of consciousness had slipped enough for him to barely notice the needle penetrating the skin and scraping past a rib. Angus was being very careful not to puncture the nerves and vessels that lay so close. Leaving the plastic cannula in place, Angus withdrew the needle and breathed an audible sigh of relief as they heard the hiss of escaping air.

Attaching the stopcock to the end of the cannula, Angus then pushed the end of the large syringe into one of the ports and the plunger moved back by itself under the pressure of air coming from the child's chest cavity. He turned off the port, emptied the syringe and repeated the procedure. This time, the plunger stopped halfway up the barrel of the syringe and Callum's small chest heaved as he coughed.

Angus grunted with satisfaction. 'I think we've got it for now, Fliss.'

'I reckon.' Fliss was watching as Callum breathed rapidly with both sides of his chest moving. She listened again with her stethoscope and nodded approval, but she still looked worried as she pulled the earpieces clear.

'How long will it last?' she wondered aloud. 'I wish we could X-ray him and get some proper drainage in place.'

'Yeah... and do an ultrasound and have a paediatric surgeon on the way?'

Fliss nodded and Angus could see the shine in her eyes that suggested tears of pure frustration were not far away. Angus ached to take her in his arms. To tell her what an amazing job she was doing. How amazing she was.

'We'll get there, lass,' he said softly. 'We're doing okay so far, aren't we?'

Fliss nodded again, blinking hard as she handed Angus some tape to secure the cannula and stopcock.

'We'll keep a close eye on him and aspirate again if we need to. Unless you've got a urinary catheter set somewhere?'

'I hadn't thought of that.' The relief was evident as Fliss realised there was something more useful they could do than simply watch. 'You're right. If we can attach the tubing to the stopcock, it could provide enough suction to draw out any new air.'

'Should keep the level down enough to prevent the lung collapsing anyway. Have you got one?'

'I think I might have. One of my elderly patients has a permanent catheter and there should be some spare supplies. I'll go and have a look in a minute.'

Callum was waking up slowly, and he was too distressed for Fliss to move away just yet.

'Where's Cody?' he begged miserably.

'We'll find him soon,' Fliss soothed. 'How's your tummy feeling?'

'It hurts.'

Despite what was obviously a very gentle touch, her examination of the child's abdomen increased his pain and he moaned.

'I want Mummy,' he sobbed. 'And Cody.'

'Abdo's not as soft as it was,' Fliss informed Angus.

He took the information on board and shared the level of concern Fliss was feeling. If the abdomen was still so painful and getting more tense, it probably meant an accumulation of blood from Callum's internal injuries. The boy was definitely the most critically ill patient they had right now.

'Could you draw up some more morphine, please, Angus? I'll check his blood pressure and we could top up his pain relief if it's not too low.'

Seth arrived beside them with the fresh oxygen cylinder and a plastic bag containing a mask. 'Sorry. It took me a while to find these. This was the smallest mask I could see. Is it what you want?'

'Yes, that's the paediatric one.' Angus took the package and ripped it open. 'Thanks, mate.'

He and Fliss worked together over the boy for several more minutes before the whimpering and calling for his brother trickled to a murmur and then stopped. With more pain relief administered and careful positioning to help his breathing, the exhausted child closed his eyes and slept.

Fliss sat back on her heels and her breath escaped in a long sigh. Angus couldn't resist touching her, but he couldn't give her the comforting hug he wanted to. He simply touched her arm so that she would know he was close.

'You remember that idea you had a while ago about making us all a hot drink?'

'Yes.' The response was dull. Looking after themselves had to be way down any list of priorities Fliss had at the moment.

'I think now might be a good time.'

'I could do with a cuppa myself.' Jack sounded suspiciously gruff and he was scrubbing beneath his eyes with the back of his hand as he stared at Callum. 'He is going to make it, isn't he?'

'He certainly will if we have anything to do with it,' Angus said firmly.

Jack nodded, his gaze now fixed on Angus. 'A wee dram might do us more good than a cup of tea,' he suggested.

Angus grinned. 'Aye. But not right now, I think. Tell you what. I'll buy you a dram when this is all over. Only when your doctor says you're well enough, mind you.'

'She's a bossy one,' Jack warned. He winked at Angus. 'There are some things a man should be able to decide for himself.'

'Aye.' Angus liked this old man.

Fliss snorted but she was checking Callum again and didn't bother joining the conversation.

'What part of Scotland are ye from, lad?'

'Edinburgh,' Angus told him, 'but I left when I was a wee lad.'

'I'm from Glasgow,' Jack said. 'And I didn't leave until I was nearly thirty, which is still a damn sight longer ago than you did.'

Fliss looked up. 'And you still haven't lost your accent, Jack.'

'I'm working on it.'

'Don't.' Fliss was smiling now. 'I love hearing it.'

Did she love his accent because it was different? Angus wondered. Or had hearing Jack possibly reminded her of himself? Fliss looked away from the old man and her gaze slipped past Angus. She looked disconcerted, as though she had just realised that she might have revealed more than she had intended.

'It's good to hear you talking properly, Jack,' Fliss said briskly. 'I think we've got your breathlessness under control for the moment.' She seemed to be avoiding looking at Angus. 'And Callum seems comfortable. I'll go and look for the catheter set and then I think I might go and make that cup of tea.'

* * *

While it was odd trying to work with only the small beam of light from the torch, it was strangely normal to be in her kitchen, filling the kettle and setting mugs and milk and a sugar bowl on a tray. It could have been just a power cut that was making the difference, rather than a full-scale emergency happening around her. Funny how quickly you could get used to things. Even while part of her brain was on full alert, waiting for more gunshots to break a now eerie silence outside, Fliss thought to unearth a packet of chocolate biscuits from her pantry and arrange them on a plate.

Not that Maria could be offered anything to eat, but a comforting, hot mug of tea probably wouldn't hurt. It could well be more than four hours before she got anywhere near the doors of an operating theatre.

Jack was highly unlikely to need an anaesthetic. He had picked up enough to make Fliss suspect that the cause of his current episode of acute heart failure was something other than a major heart attack.

Poor little Callum was in the worst shape by far and would need to be the first to be evacuated when that became possible. Fliss could only hope there weren't any others out there who might also be in dire need of medical intervention. Callum's brother Cody was the one who sprang to mind instantly. Where was he? Was it possible he had been hurt as badly as his twin? Or worse?

'Oh, God,' Fliss muttered aloud, 'I hope not.'

'What are you not hoping for?'

Fliss almost dropped the plate of biscuits. 'What are you doing in here?'

'I thought you might need a hand carrying stuff.' Angus stepped closer.

'You're a bit too good at sneaking up on people, Angus McBride.'

'Yeah?' Another step and Angus was very close to her. Close enough to touch. He smiled and Fliss felt a very familiar twist deep in her abdomen.

She had loved this man's smile from the first time she had seen it. It was kind of slow growing but it got very wide, with a cute upwards curl at the corners. It made her feel like the sun had come out from behind a cloud. Warm and... happy.

Which seemed an inappropriate way to feel, given the current circumstances. If only Angus wasn't standing close enough for her to feel his warmth, it might be easier to dampen that odd internal glow.

'I'm highly trained, you know,' Angus said quietly. 'I came top of the sneaking class.'

'Hmph.' Fliss took a step away and put the plate down on the tray. 'I hope you were top of the tray-carrying class as well. Why don't you take this? I'll bring the kettle as soon as it's come to the boil.'

Angus picked up the tray. 'You didn't answer my question.'

'What question?'

'What it was that you were not hoping for so fervently when I sneaked up on you.'

'Oh...' Fliss sighed. 'I was thinking about Callum's twin brother. Hoping that he isn't lying out there somewhere...'

She didn't need to voice the rest of her fears for Cody. The sympathetic grunt from Angus let her know he understood her concern perfectly.

He was silent for a moment and seemed to be waiting for Fliss, who was watching the curl of steam starting to come from the spout of the kettle.

'You're really close to this community already, aren't you, Fliss?'

'They're good people,' Fliss answered simply. 'It's easy to get close, especially in such a small community.'

'Don't you find it a bit stifling?'

'In what way?'

'There must be things about the city that you miss, surely?'

Was Angus asking if she missed him? This wasn't the time to start telling him just how badly she had missed him. His company, his conversation, his caring... his touch. Fliss swallowed hard.

'I miss some things.'

'Like?'

Oh, help. She had to get away from personal ground before she threw herself into his arms and burst into tears and poured out her grief. Where would that get them? Back together, probably, and back to square one. In a relationship that would eventually destroy her. She'd suffered enough already. It would be too stupid to go back for another helping. Self-destructive.

'Like not having all the facilities of a well-equipped emergency department when I need them badly,' Fliss said shortly. 'Like right now.'

'But what about the social life?' Angus persisted. 'The shopping and theatres and... and good coffee?' The whistling sound advertised that the water was hot enough, and Fliss pulled the cord free and picked up the kettle.

'I love this place,' she told Angus. 'When I was a kid we had a holiday house in a place just like this, up north. A river mouth and a beach and just a couple of shops. Miles from anywhere. We used to go for long summer holidays and Dad would take me fishing or beachcombing or walking in the forest or up the hills. It was the best place in the world.'

'Is that why you came here, Fliss?' Angus cleared his throat. 'Were things so bad that you wanted to run away to somewhere that was special when you were a kid?'

Fliss shook her head to try and deny that she had been cowardly enough to simply run away from a situation she didn't like. But that was precisely what she'd done, wasn't it? The head shake slowed and then morphed into the ghost of a nod.

'When I came here to check out the locum position I'd heard about, I knew I had to take it. I felt like I'd stepped back in time. To the best place ever. The safest place.' Fliss couldn't help the wobble in her voice. 'And I did need a safe place.'

'Was I so dangerous, Fliss?'

She couldn't answer. Couldn't tell him that it wasn't Angus himself who had been so dangerous but the way she felt about him. Being so close to losing herself, heart and soul, to someone who might walk out to go to work one day and never come back.

Like her father.

She avoided the question. 'This is a wonderful place,' she said with forced brightness. 'Ask Maria. It's the perfect place to raise a family.'

'You said you didn't want children.'

'No.' Fliss needed to push Angus away. To stop him scratching those sore patches on her soul. 'If you remember, I said I didn't want you to be the father of any children I had.'

Another moment of silence. A much heavier one. 'So...' Angus cleared his throat again. 'You're happy here, then, Fliss?'

'I was.' Forced brightness wouldn't work any longer. What was the point in being less than honest with Angus, anyway? He would see through anything less than the truth. 'Tonight changes everything, though, doesn't it? Morriston is never going to feel quite so safe after this. Maybe it was all just an illusion.'

'Maybe the degree of danger you perceive is the illusion.'

'What?' Fliss shook her head. 'There are people on the other side of that door who are full of bullet holes, Angus. That's hardly an illusion.'

She could feel the intensity of the look she was receiving even though it was too dark to see it properly.

'I wasn't talking about Morriston.'

Fliss had turned away and was already in the laundry by the time the soft words were spoken.

It was easy to pretend she hadn't heard.

6

She wasn't going to get away with it.

Angus was practically stomping as he carried the tray through the waiting area towards the surgery, and Fliss couldn't blame him. It had been a nasty dig, that comment about not having wanted *him* to be the father of her children.

It wasn't true. Of course it wasn't true. Angus had all the qualities she would have picked to be the father of her children. Strong but gentle, funny and kind. Capable of being stern but always fair. The kind of qualities her own father had had. The things that had added a much more meaningful layer to that initial physical attraction she had felt for Angus McBride.

It wasn't that she didn't want him to father her children. It was because if he *did*, with the kind of career he had, Fliss could see history repeating itself.

She would be in real danger of turning into her own mother.

And that was a path Fliss could never bring herself to take even a single step onto. She hadn't really wanted to hurt Angus – it had been self-protection. This was just *so* hard, having him so close and feeling that magnetic pull all over again. A pull towards a future that had an impenetrable barrier. A wall that hid a terrible secret. A wall that was so thick and so menacing Fliss couldn't even go near it.

In fact, she hadn't actually recognised how good she was at staying away from that wall. Maybe it was the tension of the night. Or the reminders she'd had of her past when she'd been in the cemetery earlier. Or seeing Angus again after such a long break. Or a combination of everything that was creating a very peculiar chemistry. She was suddenly closer to that wall than she had ever been in her adult life, and it was still too hard to touch.

That wall had blood on it.

It was so much less painful to create a diversion. The kind of petty things that had been so readily available when she had lived with Angus – like meals being ruined because he hadn't got home on time, or dishes not being done, or beds not being made – couldn't be used in the current circumstances, so Fliss had pulled something far more personal out of her defence armaments. One of the big guns that had been used only once before, in the final showdown before she had moved out of Angus McBride's life. At a time when she had believed what she had been feeling and saying, and hadn't been able to see it for the diversion tactic it had really been.

She couldn't afford to let herself get pushed up against that wall again. When she had time to sit down and think about it, she would be able to come up with a dozen reasons why that would be a very bad idea. Too many years had been spent creating the hard-won distance. Taking that mental journey would be impossible right now in any case, and the angry vibes coming from Angus were a huge help in creating a diversion all by themselves.

If only Fliss didn't feel guilty for the undeserved rejection that had instigated the vibes. Angus was right behind her. Fortunately, his heavy tread had not disturbed either Callum or Jack, who were both dozing comfortably.

'Where are you going to run away to next time, Fliss?'

The soft query was almost a hiss. Its tone and content were both startling enough to make Fliss pause just before they entered the surgery.

'What makes you assume I'm going to run away anywhere?'

'It's what you do, isn't it? Run away from anything dangerous? A relationship that's getting serious. A place that isn't as safe as you thought it was?' Angus was glaring at her in the dim glow of the torch. 'I never thought you were a coward, Fliss.'

That stung. If she was a coward, she'd be in Jack's cellar right now. Hiding until it was safe to come out. If Fliss needed a diversion from the real issue, that would do just fine.

'How dare you?' she muttered back. 'I put myself in as much danger as you did to try and help Maria. More, in fact. I didn't have a bodyguard with a gun watching out for *me*.'

The bodyguard with the gun was watching again now from the window, a few metres away, his eyebrows raised at the obviously acrimonious exchange. And Maria lay not far from Seth. Fliss could only hope they were being quiet enough for neither of the others to clearly hear what they were saying.

'Maybe I'm not talking about right now,' Angus said. 'There are some things you've been hiding from for most of your life. That you're still hiding from.'

Thoughts of putting the kettle down to stop the occasional wisps of stream scalding her hand were forgotten.

'Like what?' Fliss snapped.

'Like the death of your father,' Angus responded. 'You've let it poison your life, Fliss. You can't live in hiding. Not really live.'

'I intended to live,' Fliss told him, 'without taking unnecessary risks. Is that so stupid?'

'And you want a partner who feels the same way.' Angus nodded. 'Like who, Fliss? An accountant? He might get knocked off his bike on the way to work, you know. There are no guarantees in life for anybody. You have to live for every moment – you can't shut yourself away. Or shut your heart away.'

Angus sighed heavily and his anger seemed to dissipate. 'I'm sorry your dad was killed, Fliss, but you should never have let it be the end of your world.'

'You don't understand.' Fliss spoke quietly so she could be absolutely sure no one could overhear. Angus was getting too close to the real issue. And yet he was a million miles away. 'It wasn't the end. Just the beginning.'

'You're right. I don't understand. So tell me.'

Fliss hesitated but then gave her head a tiny shake and moved on towards the surgery. *Could* she tell him? Seth was staring at them both, his brow still creased with concern. Then he flattened himself against the wall and peered through the gap in the curtains again, his arms moving to hold his gun at the ready.

The tension of the night closed in again around Fliss. The edge of horror was inescapable now that they were in the surgery. How much more would it escalate before this was over?

Enough to shatter defences that Fliss had never even attempted to break? Confession was good for the soul, wasn't it? What if she died tonight and she'd never told anybody?

There was only one person on earth she would consider telling and he was walking right behind her.

'Tell me, Fliss,' he encouraged softly. 'I want to understand.'

'Fliss?'

'What is it, Maria?' Fliss glanced up at Angus, her expression intended to confirm that this wasn't the time. 'Put the tray on the desk, thanks, Angus. Maybe you could make a coffee for you and Seth.'

She stepped into the surgery properly and moved swiftly towards the bed. 'Problem?' she queried succinctly.

Maria nodded but looked embarrassed. 'I need to go to the toilet,' she whispered.

'Oh...' This was no emergency department where a nurse aide could be summoned to bring a bedpan. Fliss didn't even have such an item in the surgery, unless there was one tucked away in some dusty corner of the storage area. 'Right. I'll go and see what I can find for you to use.'

'Please... hurry.'

Fliss could see that Maria was deeply embarrassed, and no wonder! As if it wasn't bad enough to need assistance to attend to bodily functions, there were two male strangers in the same room. Fliss lowered her voice.

'I'll tuck some towels under you. Don't hang on if it's hurting. Just wet the bed.'

Maria looked agonised now. 'I think I need to... do more than that,' she whispered.

'Oh...' Again, Fliss was thrown momentarily off balance. Then she nodded decisively. There was no time to waste fossicking in the storeroom, but she had some old containers in a kitchen cupboard, including a fairly flat plastic basin. It would do and could be discarded later. 'I'll be right back.'

It took less than sixty seconds to get there and back with the item, and that included a lightning-fast check on both Jack and Callum. The young boy was still asleep but breathing well and he didn't stir as Fliss laid her hand on his abdomen. The rigidity she had feared was developing was no more advanced than it had been the last time she'd checked.

Jack was awake enough to smile at her as she flew past, and that had to be enough of an indication as to the stability of the old man's condition for now.

'You guys might need to turn your backs for a minute,' Fliss informed Seth and Angus on her return to Maria's bedside.

'Sure.' Angus was busy talking to Seth anyway.

'You got that?' Seth queried.

'No.' Angus tapped his earpiece. 'What was it?'

'There's some news coming in – we've been asked to stand by for details.'

'Dammit.' Angus tapped his earpiece again. 'I'm getting a bit of static and that's all. Can anyone hear me?'

'Try again.'

'Testing... Testing... Alpha 3 to base...'

Fliss found her mouth tightening with a hint of a wry smile. So the code name for the squad members was Alpha? How appropriate. These men were all a little larger than life. In control of their lives and, when called out, in control of everybody else's as well.

'Here we go,' she told Maria. 'This might not be very comfortable but it should do the trick. I've got a box of tissues here, too.'

'Thanks.' Maria was eyeing the men by the window.

'They won't look,' Fliss assured her.

The desk lamp angled towards the floor was still on, but it was touch rather than sight that rang the alarm bells for Fliss when she pulled back the blankets covering her patient.

The bed was soaked.

'Um... do you still feel like you need to go to the toilet, Maria?'

'Mmm.' Maria grunted. 'I can't hang on much longer.'

'Do you have any pain?'

'No. It's just really uncomfortable. Like something's pushing really hard.'

Something was indeed pushing Maria hard from the inside but it wasn't anything a simple plastic basin would be any use for.

'I think,' Fliss said carefully, 'that you might be in labour, Maria.'

'*What?* I can't be! I haven't been having any contractions or anything.'

'Are you sure? They might have been masked by the morphine you've had for your leg. Can you try and bend your good leg and shift it out a bit?' Fliss angled her torch. 'Your waters have definitely broken. Angus?'

He was by her side in a moment. He would recognise the significance of the meconium staining in the fluid-soaked sheet on the bed. Fliss didn't want to alarm Maria, but the sooner they could get this baby safely delivered, the better.

'I'll get us some gloves.'

Any embarrassment Maria had been feeling regarding any bodily functions had to be forgotten. Fliss cut away the flowered dress and Maria's underwear. This was going to be an awkward delivery anyway, with Maria having one leg anchored by a traction splint, and Fliss needed help even to gain enough access for an internal examination.

'You haven't had any ultrasound tests done during your pregnancy, have you, Maria?'

'No. I don't like doing anything unnatural that isn't absolutely necessary. And my other births have all been perfectly straightforward so I didn't think it would matter this time.' Maria drew in an anxious breath. 'Is something wrong?'

'The baby's position isn't ideal and your dilatation is asymmetrical, which isn't helping.'

'Occipitoposterior position?' Angus queried.

Fliss nodded.

'What's that?' Maria sounded more than anxious now.

'It means that the back of the head is pointing towards your back. The baby's neck has flexed so that the widest part of its head is trying to come out first.'

'You mean it's *stuck*?'

'It means that the delivery might take a lot longer than normal for you. My worry would be that the baby could be getting stressed.'

'How would you know?'

'One of the signs of stress is that meconium can be passed in the amniotic fluid.'

'And has it been?' Maria reached out to touch Fliss's arm as she sensed the hesitation. '*Tell* me, Fliss. I need to know the truth.'

'It looks like there might be some staining from meconium on the bed,' Fliss admitted. 'I'm going to listen to the baby's heart-beat now and that will be a better indication of how it's coping.'

Fliss held her breath as she moved the foetal stethoscope from one point to another on Maria's abdomen. She pressed harder. What if she didn't find one? If it was too weak to hear clearly?

If there *wasn't* one to be found any longer?

'You got that, Angus?'

'No.' Angus jerked his head towards his colleague as Fliss moved the stethoscope yet again. 'What's happening?'

'There's been a car stopped on its way to Christchurch. Apparently some high-powered weapons were found in its boot.'

'And?'

'And there it is,' Fliss said in relief as she finally located the sound of the baby's heart. She tilted her wrist and strained to see the second hand of her watch in the inadequate light as she counted the heart rate.

'And the car came over the pass. Could well have come from

here before the roads got blocked and the occupants might have just been lying low for a while.'

'They're local?'

'No.'

Maria was waiting for a verdict on her baby's condition. 'It's all right, isn't it, Fliss? It sounds a bit slower to me than the last time we listened.'

'Yes.' Fliss removed the stethoscope. 'It's down from 160 to 104, which is still in the normal range but I'd be happier if it was a bit faster.'

A slowing heart rate was another sign of potentially serious foetal distress.

'What are you going to do?'

'Don't worry.' Fliss hoped her smile was reassuring. 'Angus has probably helped with more difficult deliveries in odd places than I have. You're in good hands.'

It wouldn't be hard for Angus to be more experienced than Fliss. Babies hardly ever got born in emergency departments and it seemed far too long ago that she had done her obstetric training.

'I'm just going to go and get some towels and things,' she told Maria.

'Don't forget to boil some water.' The attempt at both a joke and a smile made Fliss return the smile more than willingly.

'Be right back,' she promised. 'Angus?'

'Yep?'

'I might need a hand.'

What Fliss really needed was another opinion. Support for what she suspected she might have to do in the very near future.

* * *

'I'm not very happy with this situation.'

Angus smiled wryly at the obvious understatement. 'How much trouble do you reckon the baby's in?'

'Too much. Maria's hardly in the best shape for this. She's fully dilated but it feels uneven.' Fliss led the way to her already depleted linen cupboard. 'There's a thickened lip of cervix anteriorly, presumably because the head hasn't been putting enough pressure in the right places. I have a feeling that if we wait and see if it's going to thin out, it's still not going to help her deliver by herself. There's already too much evidence of foetal distress, which is hardly surprising given the blood loss and stress Maria's already got.'

'What do you want to do?'

'Call an obstetrician,' Fliss snapped. 'Get a theatre on standby for an emergency Caesarean.' She shoved an armload of towels into Angus's arms. 'What do you think I want to do?'

He ignored the sarcasm. 'Find a way to deliver this baby quickly and safely,' he suggested evenly.

Fliss sighed heavily. 'Yeah... Sorry, Angus. I don't mean to take this out on you. This is just such a nightmare. I'm worried sick.'

'I know, lass.'

Fliss peered up at Angus. Maybe it was a trick of the weird lighting from using torches, but she could have sworn that if he didn't have an armload of towels, Angus would have taken her in his arms. He looked as though he wanted to kiss her. To offer support, maybe. Encouragement, perhaps. Or was it possible that he just wanted her?

Fliss dropped her gaze to the pile of towels, willing them to fall to the floor. Angus seemed to be waiting as well. Probably for her to say something that was actually relevant to the current crisis.

'I can't do a Caesarean here.' Fliss forced her brain to push any desire for physical closeness to Angus aside. 'It's totally impossible. But I'm damned if I'm going to let Maria lose this baby.'

'What about a forceps delivery?'

'A mid-cavity forceps delivery?' Fliss made an uncertain sound. 'The presenting part is only just past the ischial spine. I've only ever *watched* one, Angus. I know the theory but I'm sadly lacking in any experience. I'd have to try and rotate the head. What if I failed? I'd have distressed the baby, and Maria even more, and there'd be no surgical back-up for rescue.'

The thought of trying something that could have such disastrous consequences if it didn't go well was terrifying. But the thought of not trying anything and still getting those consequences was even worse.

'Do you have local anaesthetic?'

'Of course.'

'You're happy to do an epidural anaesthetic?'

'Yes, of course. We'd need to put one in for a forceps delivery in any case.'

'So, if the worst came to the worst, we could do an emergency Caesarean.'

We. Fliss liked that. Maybe Angus hadn't dropped the towels and gathered her close, but they were still in this together. She could feel the confidence and support Angus was exuding, and she gathered and stored it eagerly. Taking a deep breath, Fliss gave a single nod and began the short journey back to the surgery.

'You've got forceps?'

'Yes. There's an obstetric kit in the storeroom. The list I have says it contains Kjelland's forceps, but I suspect it's been years since they were used.'

'Are they in sterile packaging?'

'Yes.' Another thought occurred to Fliss as they walked past the laundry appliances, and she stopped suddenly. 'Hang on.' She turned to find Angus only inches away. 'Didn't I hear Seth talking about some guns being found?'

'Yeah. They've picked up a couple of blokes who were heading for Christchurch. A high-powered weapon was found in the boot of the car and it's apparently been used pretty recently.'

'So they're the people who were here?'

'It's possible. Probable.'

'So that means they've been caught. We could get a chopper to evacuate Maria.'

'Not yet.'

'Why not?'

'They don't know the full story. These guys are being questioned now but they're not likely to be overly co-operative.'

'But it's obvious! Who else would be trying to get away from the coast with guns?'

'It seems likely they've had a part in the incident,' Angus agreed, 'but we still don't know if there are any more outsiders involved. And we don't know where the local guy that was involved is. Darren.'

Fliss thought about this as they crossed the waiting room area. She automatically looked at the small boy lying in the corner, pausing long enough to watch his breathing for a moment.

Jack gave her a thumbs-up sign. 'I'm watching the lad,' he said. 'Sounds like you've got enough on your hands next door. I'll call you if I get worried.'

'Thanks, Jack.'

Fliss took another moment to watch the trace on the ECG screen. Callum's heart rate wasn't too fast and it appeared reassuringly even. She glanced at Angus. 'He could have been mistaken, you know – about Darren.'

'Do you really think so?'

Her head shake was disappointed. 'No. So there's no hope of evacuating anybody just yet?'

'No. Sorry. The thinking is that even if there is only one person left who's a danger, we don't have any idea where he is at the moment so it's too dangerous to allow civilian movement of any kind. They're going to start an operation to close the cordon and search until we find the offenders. They'll go through every house one by one.' Angus hesitated. 'Seth and I will probably be pulled in to help at some stage.'

'Couldn't Seth go by himself?'

'We work in pairs, Fliss.' An undertone suggested that Angus would much rather stay with her, but then he spoke more firmly. 'It's my job.'

And loyalty was one of Angus's greatest strengths. Fliss wasn't high enough on the list of where that loyalty was directed any more, was she?

'But... but what about Maria?' As childish as it seemed, Fliss couldn't help her plaintive response. 'And Jack and Callum? I... need you, Gus.'

He didn't answer. There wasn't really anything he could say, was there? Fliss could only hope that the call to take Angus away from her didn't come any time too soon.

* * *

The situation, potential complications and possible outcomes were carefully explained to Maria. She was crying by the time Fliss had finished answering all her questions, but then she sniffed hard and cleared her throat.

'Let's just get on with it, please. Put that anaesthetic in, Fliss. Use the forceps and do whatever you have to do. Just save my baby... *Please!*'

Turning Maria so that it was possible to reach her lower spine and put the epidural anaesthetic in place was a mission in itself. It was distressing for everybody, including Seth, who had to put down his gun and leave his post by the window to help hold Maria on her side.

Fliss couldn't be sure that her cannula placement was perfect given the difficulties, so it was a tense fifteen minutes or so until they realised that the nerve block had been effective.

'I can't feel my legs any more,' Maria said in surprise. 'They feel like big lumps of wood.'

Fliss swallowed hard. This was it, then. She was gowned, gloved and masked. She had the disinfectant and drapes ready, and the contents of the sterile obstetric kit had been laid out on her desk.

'I can't take that traction splint off your leg,' she warned Maria. 'I don't want to risk you losing any more blood from the fracture site. It's making space pretty tight, though, so I'll probably have to do an episiotomy.'

Maria groaned. 'That's where you cut me, right?'

'Yes. Sorry, but it's a lot better than having a tear.'

'You'll sew it up again afterwards?'

'Of course.'

Maria screwed her eyes tightly shut. 'Whatever,' she said faintly. 'I just want to get this over with.'

Fliss was ready moments later. She picked up the forceps in her gloved hands and stared at them for a moment as she extracted everything she could remember from the relevant mental files.

Kjelland's forceps had a sliding lock and minimal pelvic curve so that rotation of the forceps would not lead to damage by the blades during the process of rotation. Fliss nodded inwardly but then laid the forceps down again on the sterile drape covering her desk.

'You okay?' Angus queried softly.

The nod was obvious this time. 'I'm going to try a manual rotation first,' she told him. 'If it works, I'll use the forceps to complete the delivery.'

She was hoping, desperately, that it *would* work. Using her hand to hold and rotate the baby's head would be a lot safer than trying to cradle the tiny skull between cruel-looking metal blades.

'Okay, Maria? You might feel me pushing a bit here, but it shouldn't hurt.'

'I'm fine.'

She didn't sound fine. She sounded terrified. Fliss was aware of Angus reaching out to hold the young mother's hand, and in the fleeting instant that part of her brain registered the action, another part produced the clearest memory of exactly what Maria would be feeling. Fliss could feel it herself. The curl and grip of that big, strong hand. The gentle stroke of a thumb against a palm. Angus was very good at holding hands. So good that just the memory was enough for Fliss to be getting the same benefit Maria was right now. Enough to chase away any fear and insecurity that was blocking the total focus she needed for the challenging medical procedure she was on the point of undertaking.

A procedure that had a new life depending on it.

Whatever else was going on in the township of Morriston – even what could be happening to her other patients, out of sight in the waiting area – had to be temporarily forgotten.

The baby's head had to be turned to the anterior position through the shortest possible distance. Fortunately, with Maria's baby still three weeks away from its due date, it wasn't huge and Fliss actually found the procedure much easier than she had anticipated. She still couldn't afford to allow the delivery to continue naturally, however. When Angus located the foetal heartbeat with the stethoscope after its position had been corrected, the rate had dropped to just over eighty.

Way too slow. The baby was still in big trouble.

Fliss picked up the forceps again. She applied the left blade to the left side of the pelvis, then the right blade to the right side. She fixed the lock between the blades. Then she held her breath and concentrated on applying intermittent traction in the direction of the pelvic canal.

It seemed an agonisingly long time until a tiny head, plastered with dark hair, came into view. Anterior extension was required to effect delivery of the head and then, with a rush of fluid, the rest of Maria's baby came into the world.

'You were right, Maria! It *is* a boy!'

'*Oh*... Is he all right? Can I see him? Why isn't he crying...?'

'Can you hold the desk lamp up a bit for me please, Angus? The light's a bit low.' Fliss was amazed at how calm she sounded. She was feeling anything but calm.

One crisis had been dealt with.

Another was just starting.

There was a suction bulb from the contents of the kit on the desk. Fliss used it clear the baby's airway, but the tiny body was still limp and blue. There was no sound or movement that suggested an attempt to breathe for himself.

Prior to the delivery, Fliss had taken the precaution of laying out all the paediatric resuscitative equipment she had on hand. At the time, she had hoped it was simply a precaution. That hope evaporated as she reached for the tiny bag mask unit.

'What's wrong?' Maria sounded panicked. 'Why is he *still* not crying?'

'Give it a moment or two, love,' Angus said calmly. 'He's had a bit of a hard time getting here. He might just need a little longer to get used to things first.'

The tension was unbearable. Fliss puffed a tiny amount of air in to inflate the baby's lungs. She felt for a pulse, mentally preparing herself to start CPR and glancing towards the desk to check that the intubation gear was there. When a miniature hand suddenly jerked up a moment later and the baby screwed up his tiny features and opened its mouth to emit his first cry, Fliss found herself perilously close to tears.

Maria was sobbing aloud.

'He's *alive*... Oh, my God... I wish Ben was here.'

The baby's warbling cry strengthened. He was pinking up and his heart rate increasing. It was no longer possible to hold back tears of relief and joy when Fliss wrapped the baby in a soft fluffy towel and put him into his mother's arms. Angus sounded suspiciously gruff himself.

'He's a beauty, Maria. Congratulations.'

* * *

It seemed that only Seth was aware of a cry that wasn't coming from the newborn infant.

'Angus?'

'Yeah?'

'Can you get over here? Like, now?'

'*Help!*' Everybody heard the cry when it came again a few seconds later. 'We need help!'

'There's two people outside,' Seth said tersely.

'Dr Slade?' The banging on the door was loud. 'Are you in there? Help... *quick*! Roger's bleeding to death here.'

'Who is it, Fliss?' Angus asked. 'Do you recognise the voices?'

'Roger owns the pub. That sounds like Wayne. He's an Australian who's been working at the pub for a while.' Fliss was clamping the umbilical cord.

'Shall we let them in?' Seth asked Angus.

'I think we should—'

'Of course,' Fliss interrupted. She reached for a pair of scissors to cut the cord but glanced up, hoping to catch a glance from Angus.

She needed to let him know that she was depending on him. She couldn't cope if he left. Maybe, if she pleaded hard enough, he could defy an order to go somewhere else.

A new patient was arriving. A case that sounded like it could be critical. The Apgar score on Maria's baby might have reached an acceptable level at the five-minute point, but it still needed careful monitoring. His mother also needed attention to repair the perineal wound and deliver the placenta.

It was way past the time when Fliss would have preferred to have completed a thorough reassessment of her other two patients.

How had she ever thought she could manage without Angus McBride in her life?

She couldn't.

Not now.

Not ever.

The man was covered in blood.

'I need help,' his companion gasped. 'He can't stay on his feet much longer.'

Angus slipped his arm around the middle-aged man. 'Roger, is it? Come on, mate. Let's get you inside.'

He turned to the younger man, who had staggered to one side as he was released from the burden of supporting his injured companion. He was now leaning forward, his hands on his thighs, trying to catch his breath. 'What's happened? Has Roger been shot?'

'No...'

Fliss appeared at the door connecting the waiting area to her surgery. 'Wayne, are *you* hurt?'

'No... just Rog.'

Angus was supporting virtually all of Roger's weight, which was not inconsiderable. He felt the warmth of fresh blood well over his hand and was thankful he still had gloves on from assisting with the birth of Maria's baby.

'Got a torch, Fliss? I can't see where this blood is coming from.'

'It's his arm,' Wayne said.

'Let's get you sitting down.' Angus eased Roger to the floor, a task made easy by the way his patient's legs buckled at the suggestion. He propped the man against the wall only a few feet from Callum's bed.

Fliss was back with a torch.

'Watch the floor,' Angus warned. 'It's pretty slippery.'

With blood.

Wayne hadn't moved. 'It's his arm,' he said again.

'What happened?'

'We were trying to get away from the pub.' Wayne paused to take another ragged breath. 'Bob was worried sick about his kids.'

Bob was the father of the twins.

'He went one way and we went another... Kept ourselves hidden.'

'You didn't get challenged by the police?' Angus found the information disturbing. Two men had been moving through the township and had made it as far as the surgery without being stopped.

If they could do it, so could the man responsible for at least some of the mayhem and injuries inflicted on Morriston tonight. They were all a long way from being safe yet.

Fliss was shining the torch on Roger's upper body. Through the ragged strips of torn woollen bush shirt covering his right arm, Angus could see the blood welling.

Spurting, in fact.

'Arterial bleed.' He clamped his hand over the wound and pressed. Hard.

'We were climbing over the Daleys' back fence.' Wayne was recovering now. 'We heard something move, which turned out to be their dog, but Rog got a fright and slipped. He caught his arm on a bent bit of the corrugated-iron fence. He's been bleeding like a stuck pig ever since.'

'Roger?' Fliss crouched beside their new patient. 'Can you hear me?'

Roger nodded.

'How are you feeling?'

'Like hell,' he said succinctly.

Fliss had her fingers on his wrist. 'Still got a good radial pulse,' she told Angus, 'but we'd better get some fluids up. He's tachycardic.'

Angus nodded. He liked the way Fliss treated him as an equal when they were working together like this. Medically speaking, they made a great team, didn't they?

They would make a great team under any circumstances if only Fliss would give it a fair shot.

'I'll get the gear,' Fliss said. 'Keep the pressure on, Angus.'

He pressed harder and Roger groaned.

'Sorry, mate,' Angus said, 'but we really need to get this bleeding stopped.'

They couldn't know how much blood Roger had already lost. Having a radial pulse still present indicated that the systolic pressure was at least eighty, but it could be dropping fast and they needed to keep it up to a hundred in any case, to combat the effects of shock from lack of circulating blood volume. Silently, he willed Fliss to be speedy in getting back with the necessary equipment to start intravenous fluid replacement, but it seemed that she was going to be delayed.

'Fliss?' It was Maria calling. 'Something's happening.'

Behind him, Callum stirred and whimpered, and Angus turned his head. 'It's okay, buddy,' he called softly. 'We're still here.'

'I can look after the lad.' Jack was moving from his mattress. The old man knelt beside Callum and took hold of the young boy's hand, and Angus heard him start talking.

'I hear you're doing real well at school, young man. You have to get up early to catch the school bus, don't you? I can see you in the mornings when you and Cody are waiting at the bus stop with Mum.'

As Jack paused to catch his breath, the soft tones of Fliss's voice could be heard again, and Angus felt a familiar curl of something pleasurable deep in his gut. He loved the sound of this woman's voice.

'It's the placenta arriving, Maria. It's all fine, hun.'

The baby's cry added to the impressions Angus was getting, and Wayne was now crouched at Roger's feet.

'Is he going to be all right?'

'He's lost a fair bit of blood. I'm just trying to stop the bleeding.'

'I didn't know what to do,' Wayne confessed. 'And we were so close to the medical centre. I thought the best thing was to try and get here as fast as possible and find someone who *did* know what to do.'

'Mmm.' Angus kept his tone neutral. He couldn't blame Wayne for not wanting to stay put, and maybe he had no idea how much blood could be lost if arterial bleeding wasn't controlled.

'Roger didn't want to stop. We didn't know where that mad devil with the gun was.' Wayne dropped his voice. 'We were scared, you know?'

'I know.' It was easy to sound understanding now. Everyone was scared. Including Angus.

Scared that he and Seth would be called to rejoin their squad and take part in some containment exercise, which would mean having to desert Fliss.

What if he got injured himself?

Or worse... killed?

For the first time, Angus felt the weight of the risk his job entailed. He'd never been afraid for himself. When adrenaline was running, it was only too easy to have the 'it won't happen to me' attitude. It had never really sunk in before how something happening to him could affect someone else.

This small medical centre was turning into a circus. How on earth would Fliss be able to cope alone? But she seemed to be doing astonishingly well, and she was back by his side with a pile of intravenous supplies a very short time later.

'Placenta's arrived and appears intact,' Fliss relayed to Angus. 'I've saved it to get checked properly later.'

'How's the baby?'

'Seems fine. I've propped Maria up as much as I can with some pillows and she's managing to breastfeed him. I'm leaving the repair of the episiotomy till later when we've got more time.'

Fliss handed the torch to Wayne. 'Could you hold this, please, and point it at Roger's arm, here? I'm going to put an IV line in. Is that okay, Roger?'

'Sure.'

'I've lost track of how long I've been sitting on this.' Angus looked up at Seth. 'Any idea?'

'Must be at least ten minutes.'

'That's what I thought.'

Angus cautiously lifted his hand, but an undiminished well of blood covered the space instantly. 'Damn!' He clamped his hand back on the wound. 'It's still bleeding, Fliss.'

'Mmm.' Fliss had her head bent, intent on inserting a wide-bore cannula in Roger's other forearm. 'We might need to try and tie off that artery.'

Her movements were swift and efficient as she taped the cannula into place, attached the giving set and the bag of fluids.

'Could you be a pole, please, Wayne? If you can squeeze the bag and get the fluids to go in a little faster to start with, that would be great.'

Fliss wrapped a blood-pressure cuff where the loose tourniquet was still in place. Then she pulled the stethoscope from around her neck. 'I'll just get a quick BP and then I'd better change Callum's fluids.' She hesitated for a moment. 'I took the bag of saline from your kit, Gus. I've run out of extras now.'

Only Angus and Fliss were aware of the significance of her comment. Fluids were their main weapon in fighting to keep these patients stable until they could get them to hospital. Especially for Callum.

Jack was still having his one-sided conversation with the boy.

'That's a pretty smart bike you've got, lad. You and Cody got them for your birthday a while back, didn't you?'

The object of the old man's devoted attention stirred and they all heard the low moan.

'Cody-y...'

Roger twisted his head to look at Callum. His pale face folded into distressed lines and then he looked up at Fliss.

'He's hurt bad, isn't he?'

'I'm afraid so.'

'Where's the other one? Cody?'

'We don't know.'

Angus could hear the fear in her voice. He wanted to tell her things were going to be all right – that Callum would make it to hospital and an operating theatre in time and that they would find his twin and reunite the brothers – but he couldn't say that, could he?

He wanted to storm out into the night and end the terror for everyone, especially for Fliss. But he couldn't do that either.

Or could he?

Seth was obviously getting a message through on his radio. Angus could hear the buzz of static on his own malfunctioning equipment.

'We've got a rendezvous point,' Seth told him when the static cleared. 'We're due there in ten minutes. The guys they picked up in the pass have admitted there are other members of the gang still here. They've also revealed that the agenda was to deal with both the Barrett brothers and the younger guy that was involved in the dealing. Two people have been spotted on the move and, assuming that Darren is alone, they have to be gang members. We're closing the cordon and clearing each house on the way in.'

'How far away is the rendezvous?'

'We should leave now.'

Angus shook his head. 'I can't leave *now*!'

Seth gave him a very level look but said nothing.

'For God's sake.' Angus knew where his duty lay and he wasn't about to shirk the responsibilities that came with his career, but this was impossible. 'My hand is the only thing that's stopping this man bleeding to death.'

Seth looked at Wayne. He looked back at Angus and raised his eyebrows meaningfully. Fliss had another able-bodied man to help her, didn't she?

Angus was needed elsewhere.

'I'm going to find a clamp and some sutures.' Fliss scrambled to her feet. 'We'll have to get this artery sorted. Can you stay and help for just a few more minutes, Gus? Please?'

The plea tore at Angus. He had a duty to go with Seth and

strong loyalty to his squad members, but the loyalty he felt for Fliss outweighed anything else at this moment.

'Buy us a bit of time?' he asked Seth. 'It's important, mate.'

'I'll see what I can do.' Seth didn't sound happy. He'd spent the last few hours on little more than sentry duty. Of course he wanted to get out there and in on the action. It was what they trained for. The kind of opportunity they'd curse missing if they hadn't been on duty.

He wanted to be part of the operation that would bring this incident to a close. An operation that could well involve some very serious tactics, like the use of teargas or stun grenades or firearms. The kind of action the squad trained for so assiduously and rarely got to put into practice for real.

Fliss clearly realised the significance of asking for the delay. She was moving fast. She laid out a suture kit, stripped off her gloves and donned a fresh pair. She drew up local anaesthetic and gave Wayne directions as to where they needed the strongest beam of light from the torch.

'I'm going to put in as much local as I can,' she told Roger, 'but this is going to hurt. I'm sorry.'

'Do what you need to, Dr Slade. I don't want to bleed to death.'

'You're not going to.' Angus kicked himself mentally for having scared Roger, but Seth wouldn't have been impressed by anything less than the truth. He shifted a pile of gauze swabs closer. He had to try and keep pressure on the artery and keep his fingers away from the needle as Fliss infiltrated the area with local. Then he needed to keep them away from the scalpel as she cleaned torn flesh obscuring the wound. He also had to try to swab blood fast enough for Fliss to see what she was doing.

'Right. Take the pressure off,' Fliss instructed Angus only a minute or two later.

Blood welled instantly and the torchlight wavered as Wayne groaned.

'Keep it steady, Wayne. You're doing a brilliant job there.' Fliss had artery forceps in her hand. She pushed them into the gaping wound as Angus removed a newly soaked swab. He heard the clicking as the clamp tightened. He swabbed again, reached for a fresh swab immediately to repeat the procedure, but it wasn't needed.

'We've got it,' Fliss said almost gleefully. 'Now, where's that suture?'

With the artery firmly tied off, it would be possible to dress the wound and bandage it, but they didn't get that far. As Fliss flushed the area with saline, she was suddenly knocked off balance.

Jack, who had been just behind her as he reassured Callum, had simply stopped in mid-sentence and toppled sideways.

'What the—' Fliss dropped the saline pouch and pushed herself upright to her knees. 'Jack? *Jack?*'

'Hell,' Wayne said in horror. 'What's happened to him?'

'He might have fainted at the sight of all that blood.' Angus was rolling the old man onto his back. He tilted Jack's head back to open his airway, laid his hand on the elderly man's abdomen and put his own cheek close to Jack's mouth, silently pleading that this was just a vagal episode.

The plea was in vain.

'He's not breathing,' Angus informed Fliss tersely.

Fliss seemed frozen for a moment, as though this latest crisis was the last straw. Her ability to cope had reached its limit.

'Grab a bag mask,' Angus suggested calmly. He had his fingers on the side of Jack's neck now. There was no pulse to be felt. 'I'll get the lifepack off Callum.'

Jack still had electrodes in place from his earlier monitoring, so it took only seconds to get a reading of the cardiac activity.

'Coarse VF,' Angus told Fliss.

'We might still be in time, then.' She was moving again now. Fast. She held the bag mask over Jack's face and inflated his lungs rapidly. Once. Twice.

Angus cut Jack's shirt completely clear. He stuck on the defibrillator pads and reached to hit the charge button on the lifepack.

'Charging to maximum joules,' he announced. 'Stand clear.'

'I'm clear,' Fliss responded. She was pulling at the contents of Angus's kit, finding the intubation gear in its separate roll. As Angus delivered the first shock and then immediately started chest compressions, she pulled the oxygen tubing from Callum's mask and attached it to the bag mask unit. Before Angus completed the two-minute cycle of compressions when they could shock his heart again, she was ready to intubate.

'Give me some cricoid pressure, please, Gus.'

Angus pressed down on Jack's Adam's apple. He glanced at the lifepack screen where he could see that the fatal arrhythmia was reducing in amplitude. This was not looking good but that was hardly unexpected. Jack was old. He had a heart that had already been struggling for goodness knew how long. A new infarction or possibly an extension of whatever had caused the earlier episode of acute heart failure was highly likely to be irreversible.

But Fliss was clearly determined that it wouldn't be. 'Thank goodness he's got IV access already.' She had listened to Jack's chest with the stethoscope as she'd inflated the bag mask to check that the endotracheal tube was correctly positioned to protect his airway.

Now she was reaching inside the kit again. 'Where's your adrenaline? And syringes?'

'Top pocket.' Angus moved around Fliss to start chest compressions from over Jack's head so he could manage the ventilations at the same time. Then he changed his mind.

'Why don't you do the compressions?' he suggested. 'It'll be faster for me to find the drugs.'

'Angus?' Seth was standing beside Wayne, who was holding the torch in a noticeably shaking hand.

Angus gave him only a brief glance. He and Fliss were busy here. 'Yeah?'

'Operation Springclean is under way. We're needed.'

In the split second of astonished silence that followed Seth's tense comment, Angus could hear the muffled sound of what was probably a stun grenade going off. He looked at Fliss, the long tendrils of now damp blonde hair swinging beside a face set into the grimmest lines he'd ever seen as she pushed down on Jack's chest.

'Twenty-nine... thirty...' She sat back on her heels, picked up the bag mask and squeezed two breaths into Jack's lungs. Then she dropped the bag mask, got back up to her knees, leaning over his head as she positioned her hands on his sternum, and began compressions again. 'One... two...'

Angus ignored Seth. He injected another dose of adrenaline. He pressed the charge button again.

'Stand clear, Fliss,' he ordered, seconds later.

Fliss wriggled backwards, holding her hands up in front of her in a gesture of surrender. 'I'm clear.'

Angus delivered the shock. He knew that Seth was now furious. That he *had* to obey orders and go but couldn't leave his partner. That he thought this was a funny-looking, old, sick man and they were wasting their time trying to save him.

They probably were, but Fliss had a tear running down

beside her nose as she sat back and watched Jack's body jerk from the shock, and it ripped a hole in his own heart.

This was where he really needed to be. With Fliss. Not out there in the dark, scrambling around in an armed-offender operation with a cute name, waiting for someone – possibly himself – to be shot at.

Why had he ever thought he needed that kind of a thrill as part of his job?

No wonder it had frightened Fliss that he wanted to go and do something like this.

And why had it frightened her?

Because she was afraid of losing him.

And why had she been so frightened of losing him?

The only reason could be that she loved him. *That* much.

He drew up another dose of adrenaline and injected it.

It should be suffocating that someone loved you that much. It *had* been. Angus had rebelled. Hadn't even given head space to the possibility that the antipathy Fliss had displayed had been reasonable.

It didn't seem suffocating now, though.

It felt protective. Nurturing.

Perfectly understandable. It was exactly the way he'd feel about Fliss if she wanted to go and do something dangerous.

'Charging again. Stand clear.'

No. Angus didn't need the thrill of getting out there and getting shot at. The kind of challenge and satisfaction he'd got from working with Fliss in the surgery tonight was more than enough, and he could get that kind of thrill from an ordinary job as a paramedic out on the road in a large enough city.

He *could* compromise on his career.

Fliss might consider moving back to the city. She missed working in an emergency department – she had admitted that.

And look at what he would gain instead of the thrill of dramatic incidents. Wouldn't being with Fliss for the rest of his life more than make up for any excitement he lost in his career?

Yes. It would.

The screen had cleared from the disruption of the last shock.

The flat line of asystole they could see said it all.

There was no point in continuing the resuscitation effort.

Jack was dead.

Fliss sat like a stone for several seconds. Then, very slowly, she got to her feet. She turned and walked away. Through the connecting door that led to her house. She closed the door behind her quite calmly.

'*Angus!*' The command from Seth was laced with urgency.

Angus jumped to his feet.

'You go,' he told his partner. 'I can't. Not just yet.'

And he, too, turned and walked through the door into the house.

8

The bitter gall of failure threatened to choke her.

Fliss shoved the connecting door shut behind her and then hung over the laundry tub, dry-retching.

In the space of a few short hours her life seemed to have spun in on itself. She was being sucked back to a place she couldn't bear to go. Tension and now grief combined to hammer her to a point so low she couldn't get up.

She was past her breaking point.

She couldn't help anybody else.

Fliss couldn't even help herself.

* * *

She didn't hear the door open. She could feel the iron-hard muscles in the hands and then the arms that pulled her up and held her. She was aware of the voice and the deep rumble of support.

Of love.

The words were incomprehensible, but that made no difference. No amount of support – or even love – could take away the dark weight suffocating Fliss. Words were coming from her own mouth as well, equally indistinguishable because they were carried on a tide of racking sobs. Sounds torn from her soul.

Grief for Jack.

Grief for her mother.

Admission of the failure that had shaped her whole life. Time ceased to exist. It could have been minutes or hours but was probably only seconds until the words began to make sense.

Words from Angus.

Words from herself.

Words she had never thought she would hear herself utter.

'You're not a failure, Fliss.'

'I *am*.'

'No. You did your best.'

'It wasn't good enough.'

'Jack was an old man. He was sick. Nobody could have done anything more. Nobody could have saved him.'

'I tried.'

'I know you did, love.'

'I tried so hard, Gus… and I couldn't do it.'

'I know. I'm so sorry.'

'I tried for years.'

'No… you've only been here a little while, Fliss. You can't take responsibility for what went before.'

'Years and years and years. I tried everything but I couldn't know, could I? I was only ten.'

The arms held her tighter.

'Ten? You mean when your dad died?'

'I couldn't see it starting. Maybe if I'd done something differently… if I'd been older and could see what was happening.'

'I don't understand, Fliss.'

'No. Nobody could ever understand.'

'I could. Tell me.'

'You'd hate me.'

'I could never hate you.'

'I hate myself.'

'Why?'

'Because... because I *failed*.'

'*How* did you fail, Fliss?'

'My... mother...' A cry that felt like it was taking part of her lungs with it was cushioned by the chest Fliss had her face buried against. 'She killed herself, Gus.'

There was a moment's shocked silence.

'It was my fault,' Fliss sobbed.

'*No!*' Angus spoke so vehemently the negation was almost believable. 'I don't believe that.'

'It's true. I failed. I could have found a way to help and I didn't. I didn't know how.'

'Of course you didn't. You were a child.' A hand moved to cradle the back of her head. To stroke her hair. 'What happened, lass? Why did your mother take her own life?'

'Because Dad wasn't there any more.' Fliss hiccupped and pulled out another shard that had pierced her heart so long ago. 'Because she loved him more than anyone in the world. Because it wasn't enough having me to live for.'

'Oh, sweetheart...' His lips were on her hair as well now. And then Angus bent his head further to press his cheek to the top of her head. 'I don't believe that, either. Not for a second.'

'It's true. Of course it's true. She left me, didn't she? She left me *forever*.' The sobs hurt so much. They were pulling out a long-buried pain and it hadn't lost any of its intensity for having been kept out of sight for so long. 'Why would she do that, Gus?'

'It wasn't your fault, my love.'

'She was one of those people who liked everything to be perfect, you know?' Fliss gulped in air as the words started tumbling out. 'The house was always so tidy and she'd put fresh flowers everywhere. Flowers that she grew in her own garden. She cooked wonderful meals and... and there was always a water jug with ice in it on the table. She even used to freeze mint leaves inside the ice blocks.'

'Mmm.' The sound was simply encouragement.

'But it was never over the top, you know? It made her happy. She used to sing all the time. She wanted everything to be perfect for Dad because she loved him *so* much. More than she loved me.'

'No.' Angus was rocking her gently. 'Not true, Fliss.'

'When Dad was killed, the sun went out for her. She never picked flowers any more. She never even pulled out any weeds in the garden. I tried... but I couldn't tell the difference between the flowers and the weeds. And I tried to keep the house tidy. I tried to learn to cook but the only thing I knew how to do was scrambled eggs.'

'She was depressed,' Angus said. 'She needed more help than a child could give her.'

'She tried pills. All sorts of pills. They tried putting her in a hospital but it was never enough. And one day, just before I turned fourteen, I came home from school and found her...'

Fliss took a deep, shaky breath. 'She'd taken all the pills she had in the house, Gus, and she hadn't... hadn't even written me a letter to say... to say goodbye.'

Fliss was still being held, still gently rocked. Words of comfort and reassurance flowed over her and finally, as the pain and her distraught weeping ebbed away, the words started to have a real effect. To impart a new strength. Something so new and so wonderful Fliss was scared to try and name it.

The rap on the door was jarring.

'Angus? *Now*, mate. I can't wait any longer. I'm going.'

'I can't go,' Angus said.

Fliss shook her head. 'You can't stay, Gus. Not on my account. You're here to do a job. *Your* job.'

'I'm needed here, too. Seth can join the others without me. You can't manage by yourself in there. Not after... Jack.'

The new strength was still there. Growing, even, thanks to the concern in Angus's voice and the way he was holding her arms and trying to see her face in the edge of the light from Seth's torch.

'I can manage,' she said bravely. 'I've got my job to do, too. And I've got Wayne to help me.' She took a deep breath, and it wasn't shaky this time. 'I won't fall apart again.'

She knew she was speaking the truth. There was actually a curious calm to be found now in the aftermath of that emotional storm. More than the tension of this night that had been released for her in the last few minutes. More than the aftermath of breaking up with Angus. Ancient ghosts had been recalled and, for the moment anyway, seemed to have been laid to rest.

Of course it hadn't been her fault that her mother had chosen not to live. Sadly, not everyone could be saved. She had seen that too often in her career, with the most recent demonstration still painfully raw.

She wasn't unlovable.

Angus loved her.

He knew the worst of her now and he was still there. Still caring. Caring enough to risk his career because *she* needed him.

Fliss straightened her back and managed to twist her mouth into something surprisingly close to a smile. 'Hardly the best time or place to dump on you, was it? Sorry.'

'Don't be. We're going to talk about this again, Fliss. Very soon.'

Seth made a sound like a growl and then turned on the heel of his boot and strode away.

'Okay, okay, I'm coming.'

Angus let go of Fliss and stepped back, his reluctance evident in his hunched shoulders and rigid back. He got through the door of the laundry and a second later his huge body filled the gap again. A swift step towards Fliss and his hands gripped her arms. He bent his head and planted one swift, firm kiss on her lips.

'I love you, Fliss,' Angus said urgently. 'Always have, always will.'

Then he was gone again.

And this time Fliss knew he wouldn't be coming back.

Fliss had to move, too. She couldn't afford to stand here in the dark and think about what had been the most intimate conversation she'd ever had with Angus.

Or think about the way he'd held her. The feeling it had given her of being whole. Of finding a strength she'd never known existed.

Most of all, Fliss couldn't afford to give heart or head space to the terrible fear that had come as Angus had disappeared through the door that second time.

The fear that she would never see him again.

She hadn't even had time to echo his words. He couldn't hear her now, but she whispered them aloud anyway.

'I love you, too, Gus. Always have. Always will.'

* * *

He'd had *no* idea.

That Fliss had adored her father had always been obvious. She'd kept a photograph in pride of place beside her bed. A picture Angus had seen many, many times. It was an informal snap of a young, laughing girl standing behind a large, male version of herself. Her arms were draped over his shoulders and the photographer had caught a moment when they'd both turned to catch each other's gaze and share a probably private joke. The bond and depth of love between father and daughter had been as sharply defined as the corners of the frame holding that image.

Angus had always assumed that the antipathy Fliss had towards him doing a job that carried a risk greater than most careers was due to the fact that her beloved father's presence had been torn from her life in such an untimely fashion. That she'd never got over his death and that was why he was never far from her thoughts and dropped into conversations so often.

'This way.' Seth's instruction was curt. He had waited for Angus because protocol meant they had to work in pairs, but he had been infuriated by the delay. 'They've cleared all dwellings on Jasmine Lane. We've got a new rendezvous point on the corner of Seaview and Camp roads. We need to cover ground a bit faster.'

Angus obediently jogged close behind Seth, but he felt cut off from what was happening around him on more than one level. His radio was dead so he was missing communication between squad members, but he could imagine what was happening thanks to the hours of training with the men from the police department's special operations section.

The cordon was closing. Each house was being checked. Occupied houses were being approached very cautiously so that squad members could identify themselves and reassure people that the situation was under control and that somebody would come and tell them as soon as it was safe to leave their homes.

Apparently, unoccupied houses would be approached with even more caution. The potential for attack by an armed offender was high. Empty houses had to be made as safe as possible for searching, which was where the stun or teargas grenades could be deployed, but using such resources on terrified and innocent citizens that might be hiding inside their own houses was unacceptable. The operation would be slow moving and tense.

And Angus couldn't seem to summon the level of adrenaline needed to keep him focused and involved in what was going down. He was cut off by more than a lack of contact with his colleagues. He didn't want to be doing this right now.

He wanted to be with Fliss.

Holding her.

Listening to her. The revelation about her mother had been stunning. It had never occurred to Angus to wonder why Fliss had never really spoken about her. Why there had been no photographs. Again, he had made an assumption that her father had been the more important figure in her life and the impact of his death had magnified his position.

Beneath those few, choked words Fliss had spoken tonight had clearly been a deep love. Anguish at losing her mother as well as her father. Not a clean cut either. The wound had festered slowly for years, leaving a vulnerable teenager feeling bewildered, abandoned, unworthy and ultimately guilty.

The scars would run deep but Angus wasn't afraid to take them on. To help Fliss heal.

What else could he do? He loved her. That love had only increased with the understanding of why Fliss had been so afraid. Why she'd seen no future for them. And why she'd said what she had about not wanting him to be the father of her children.

She'd seen what happened to a loving family when a father's sacrifice for the career he'd loved had been too great. On an instinctive level, Fliss had every reason to fear that she wouldn't be able to cope any better than her mother had. Every reason to fear for what their children might have to go through.

She knew that pain only too well.

Right now, Angus could feel it too. He needed to be by the side of the woman he loved. To coax that child within to show her tear-stained face again so that he could at least start to try and kiss it better.

The need was so strong, Angus found himself turning to look in the direction from which they had just come.

'Gus – get down!'

A rough hand grabbed him and Angus found himself sprawling on the side of the gravel road. Rolling under the prickles of a hawthorn hedge as a single shot rang out.

Loud enough to hurt his ears.

Close enough for him to actually hear the horrible scream of a high-velocity bullet as it went past, inches from his head – through the hedge and into a window of a nearby house, where the glass shattered with a bang that seemed to echo the gunfire.

Angus didn't need Seth's hand pressing on his back to remind him to keep his head down. He couldn't afford to think about Fliss any more. He had to focus completely if he wanted to get out of this alive.

And he had to get out alive because otherwise he would never see Fliss again.

* * *

The doors were locked.

The curtains on the windows were drawn shut.

The light was still a muted glow from the desk lamp on the floor.

Nothing had changed as far as the available security for the people within the small medical centre of Morriston was concerned, except that Angus and Seth were no longer there.

But that was enough to make Fliss feel totally exposed. Very, very afraid. More vulnerable than she had ever felt in her entire life.

Or had that moment come when Angus had told her he loved her and she hadn't had the time to respond?

What if she never saw him again?

If she could never, ever feel as whole as she had when he had held her while she'd shared some of that dark cloud that had always hung over her?

Fliss wasn't afraid for her own physical safety.

She was afraid for Angus.

She was also deeply concerned for the people in her care who were obviously feeling the vacuum left by the departure of what had, effectively, been an armed guard.

Just as obviously, Fliss had been left in command.

'What would you like me to do?' Wayne was crouched beside Roger, who was staring at Jack's body with an expression where horror and disbelief were still in conflict.

'Help me move Jack,' Fliss said quietly. 'We'll put him back on his mattress and I'll find a blanket to cover him.'

The living needed her attention more, but Fliss had to take just a minute or two out of respect for this brave old man. She removed the ugly tube still protruding from his mouth and couldn't help shedding another few tears as she smoothed the beard, still blackened with boot polish. Jack had been on her side from the moment she'd arrived in Morriston, hadn't he?

He'd made her feel welcome. Needed. He'd supported her to the best of his ability. Far more than he'd needed to as far as tonight's circumstances had dictated. Would he still be alive now if he hadn't pushed himself to help her? Callum probably wouldn't be. Fliss would make sure that everybody in Morriston knew how heroic Jack's last hours had been.

She closed Jack's eyes, removed the electrodes stuck to his chest and took out the IV line in his arm. Then she gently drew a blanket over the first patient she had seen in this small community, knowing that she was drawing a curtain over a phase in her life that was rapidly coming to an end.

Having been with Jack when this terrible night had begun – when that first shot had been heard – made it somehow fitting that another shot rang out as she draped the blanket over Jack's face and shut his body away from the world for the moment.

Wayne leapt to his feet and swore vehemently. Then he gave Fliss an apologetic glance. 'That was bloody close,' he added by way of an excuse.

Fliss simply nodded. 'Stay with Roger,' she said calmly. 'Stay sitting down and keep your heads below the level of the windows.'

'Won't do any good if he decides to break in.'

'He won't.'

'How do you know that?'

'The police are closing in on him. He's shooting in self-defence.'

She didn't voice the thought that Darren could possibly be shooting to try to escape being cornered. If the effects of mind-altering drugs had worn off, he might realise what he'd done and take the only escape route available. And maybe suicide was the preferable option.

At least that way Angus would be safe.

No. Fliss shook her head as she moved to Callum and crouched beside the small boy. Suicide could never be the best answer to anything.

The multiple, rapid shots that came in response to the single retort they had heard suggested that things were far from finished in Morriston. More than one person was out there, possibly trying to stave off capture and arrest. They were clearly prepared to do battle with the authorities and they had already proven their lack of consideration for any consequences of random shooting.

Fliss reattached the electrodes to the lifepack, which was no longer needed by Jack. A red light was flashing to warn that battery power had been largely depleted by the energy used in trying to restart the old man's heart. Fliss could only hope they would hold out for monitoring duties because it would take hours to recharge them.

Callum stirred and whimpered, and Fliss smoothed back his hair. 'It's okay, sweetheart,' she murmured. 'It'll all be over soon.'

'Cody-y...'

Oh, God. Fliss had forgotten about Callum's missing twin. Had he been within range of the latest volley of shots they'd heard? Could the small boy have been caught in the crossfire – as Maria had been? Her head was too full of fear for others right now. Especially the fear she had for Angus. The level of tension was enough for Fliss to be aware of a slight tremor in her hands as she reached for Callum's wrist. What she needed to do was to focus and look after her patients.

It was impossible to push Angus away completely, though. Fliss watched the rhythm on the screen of the lifepack, her fingers on Callum's wrist to check the quality of his pulse, and she could remember how it felt to have her cheek resting on Angus's chest – feeling the steady beat of *his* heart. His life.

Was that heart still beating? Was he safe?

Callum's heart rate had increased slightly, but it was steady and his radial pulse strong enough to reassure Fliss that his blood pressure was within acceptable limits. His breathing was also steady. No need to try to drain any more air from his chest cavity.

Angus had performed that procedure so competently. He'd been so gentle with the boy. He'd be a wonderful father.

How could Fliss have been cruel enough to tell him she didn't want him to be the father of *her* children?

What if he was killed tonight and his last memory of her was those words instead of what she should have told him before he'd left?

That she loved him.

So much.

The bag of IV fluid running into Callum and helping to keep his blood pressure up was well past half-empty. Fliss turned the rate down to make it last a little longer and reminded herself to keep a close watch on his blood pressure from now on.

Roger needed more fluids but there were no new bags of saline to replace the empty one. Fliss turned the wheel on the line to shut off the connection before blood could start backing up the line in the vacuum.

'How are you feeling, Roger?'

'Bit sick. Dizzy. My arm hurts.' Roger glanced across at the shrouded figure of Jack and he swallowed hard. 'I'm okay,' he amended soberly.

Fliss moved into the surgery where Maria was cradling her newborn. She thought about stitching Maria's episiotomy wound, but that slight tremor she could still feel in her hands could mean the result would be less than perfect, and that wouldn't be good enough. The wound was covered with a damp gauze pad and the epidural was still effective enough to keep Maria comfortable. That repair could be done at the same time as the surgery she would need on her leg.

Maria clearly wasn't thinking about any medical procedures she still needed. She was completely focused on her newborn and the baby was staring back up at his mother with intent, wide-open eyes.

'That noise didn't bother him at all.' Maria sounded curiously calm herself, given that she would have recognised the sound of the gunshot for what it was. 'Isn't he an angel?'

'He's gorgeous.'

'I can't wait for his dad to meet him. And the girls.'

'He'll probably get his photo in the papers. He'll be famous.'

'Why?'

'Not many babies get born under siege conditions. Not in this country anyway.'

'No.' Maria smiled wryly. 'It'll be something to remember, won't it? Nobody's going to forget the night this little one was born.'

Fliss smiled back. She would certainly remember this birth for the rest of her life. A moment of joy amidst fear and tragedy. Something to hang on to.

If Angus didn't come back, what memories would she cling to of him? That moment of closeness in the laundry? The early days of being so passionately in love?

She could have had so many more memories, couldn't she, if she hadn't wasted the last three months of her life by being apart from Angus?

Would it make it any easier not to have extra memories to agonise over? Close moments that would stand out and make her miss him even more?

No. She would have treasured those moments. Jewels that could be used, in time, for comfort. Like the memories she had of her father. Of him taking her fishing, telling her the names of the trees and birds in a forest, watching a dragonfly settle on her extended hand for an instant and having her fear turn to excitement at her father's smile.

There had to be more moments for Fliss to collect with Angus.

She simply couldn't bear it if there weren't.

Like a drum roll to emphasise the significance of her thoughts, a volley of shots rang out. Shots that had to be coming from more than one weapon, given the variation in their sound and timing.

'Sounds like some sort of battle going on,' Wayne said nervously.

'Must've found the bastards,' Roger suggested.

Maria held her baby closer and closed her eyes as though sending up a silent prayer for their safety.

Fliss stood very still. Frozen by the fear generated from knowing that Angus was out there somewhere. Probably in the midst of all that shooting.

It was all too easy to allow that fear to become so much more personal. To admit how devastating it would be not to see Angus again.

If something happened to him, Fliss would lose the man she loved. The future she really wanted would no longer be available to her.

And no alternative could ever be good enough to make up for that.

9

The silence was deafening.

Within the walls of Morriston's medical centre, everyone seemed to be holding their breath. The sounds of gunfire had reached a crescendo and then stopped. Suddenly. As though it had been a scene being filmed for a movie and the director had chopped the air with his hand and yelled, 'Cut!'

Was it over?

Had Darren been found? Cornered? Shot dead or arrested? Or had he managed to escape and was now moving under the last stretch of darkness this night could provide?

What would happen next?

Fliss was the first to break the silence as she moved to check on all those under her care.

'Maria? You okay?'

Maria was crying. Clutching her newborn son so tightly that he began wailing in protest. Fliss wrapped her arms around both of them.

'It's all right, love. It must be over now. Hang in there.'

They'd hear something soon, surely? Someone in a uniform would come to tell them it was safe to leave. Safe to evacuate these patients to the definitive medical care they needed.

Maybe that someone would be Angus. And Fliss would be close enough to him to try to convey how she felt – with just a look or a touch, until they could find time to be alone and talk to each other. The sooner that moment could come, the better.

She knelt beside Callum again, running through all his vital sign measurements. Blood pressure, heart rate and rhythm, breathing pattern and rate. Nothing had changed dramatically but Fliss could feel the kind of prickle on the back of her neck that she'd felt when this had all started. Back when she'd been standing in Jack's kitchen before the first shot had even been fired.

When she'd known something wasn't right. That something dreadful was out there – just waiting to show itself.

She was feeling it again and Fliss frowned deeply as she gazed at the unconscious young boy. Was the new potential disaster that Callum was going to crash and there would be nothing she could do about it? She wouldn't even be able to run a resuscitation protocol now because the batteries on the lifepack had been flattened by their attempt to save Jack.

A futile attempt, but Fliss couldn't allow herself to be drawn back into that grief.

'Roger? How are you feeling?'

'Bloody terrified,' the owner of the Hog responded. 'What the hell is going to happen next?'

'Rescue,' Fliss said firmly. 'But right now I'm going to get a proper dressing on that arm of yours. I'd hate you to get an infection on top of everything else.'

It was good to have something practical and easy to do like

cleaning a wound and dressing it – at least that was something she could still do competently, despite that annoying tremor that wouldn't go away.

Wayne was shaking a lot more than Fliss was. He seemed young and vulnerable enough to tug at her heart strings almost as much as Callum did. She looked up from positioning the sterile pad over the open flesh on Roger's upper arm.

'How are you doing, Wayne?' Fliss smiled at Roger's employee. 'You all right?'

He swallowed hard and then tried to return her smile. 'I thought backpacking around New Zealand might be an exciting thing to do for a year or so. I had no idea!'

'It's never been this exciting before.' Roger shook his head. 'I think I should pack my bags and head back to the city after this.'

'And I should've stayed home,' Wayne said. 'Gone to varsity instead of having a gap year.'

Fliss could detect something beneath the young man's obvious fear. A kind of excitement or exhilaration at being part of something so dangerous. The kind of buzz that could grow to be an attraction. Was it a macho thing? Part of what had driven Angus into the career he loved?

'How old are you, Wayne?'

'Nineteen,' he told her.

'And what are you planning to do at university?'

'Haven't really thought about it yet. I wouldn't mind being a doctor after watching you tonight.'

'Not as exciting as being a cop. Or a paramedic.'

'Yeah.' Wayne's smile was much brighter this time. 'Those guys are something else, aren't they? I'd love to do the kind of job Angus does.'

'Yeah.' Fliss echoed his agreement as she taped the end of the bandage securely around Roger's arm. Then her head turned swiftly towards the door. 'What was that?'

'What?' The two men looked in the same direction.

'I thought I heard something. Listen.'

The sound came again. Louder this time. A vehicle of some sort was moving nearby. Then came the sound of heavy doors slamming, boots scraping rapidly in gravel and finally a loud rap on the door of the medical centre.

'Police,' a voice shouted.

'And ambulance,' another voice said. 'You still in there, Dr Slade?'

Fliss turned to find both Wayne and Roger staring at her. Waiting. Giving her the power to end this nightmare for them all by acknowledging rescue and unlocking the door still keeping the rest of the world at bay.

She found her legs distinctly wobbly as she moved to do exactly that, and it was hard to return the smile she received from John, a local paramedic she had met on more than one occasion.

'You all right, Dr Slade?'

'I'm fine, thanks, John.'

'I'm Detective Inspector Ross Stringer.' The man beside John introduced himself. 'Do you have any patients needing urgent evacuation?'

The senior police officer was frowning as he took in the sight of Callum, the lifepack beside him with an empty bag of IV fluid draped over its handle. His frown deepened as he shone his torch on the mattress beside the young boy.

'You've had a fatality?'

'Yes.'

'Gunshot wound?'

'No. Probably a heart attack. An elderly patient of mine who was unwell before any of this started.' Fliss turned to speak to the paramedic. 'The most urgent evacuation is Callum here. He's six years old and has an abdominal gunshot wound. He developed a tension pneumothorax which has been treated but he's in shock. His blood pressure's not stable and I'm out of fluids. Have you got some saline with you at the moment?'

'The truck's outside.' John directed his partner to fetch the required supplies. 'We've got a helicopter on standby on the other side of the bridge. Callum's father is there, too. I heard him trying to persuade someone to let him come back.'

Fliss could understand the desperation. 'His brother is still missing. He was with Callum when he was injured.' She caught Ross Stringer's gaze again. 'Do you know anything about anyone else who's out there? Injured? Do I need to see anyone?'

The detective inspector shook his head. 'Not as yet. We've got a fatality near the river mouth. Middle-aged man. There's another body being retrieved at sea. A couple of minor injuries reported from houses that have been cleared but they're being treated at the first-aid station. There's a lot of people not accounted for yet.' He shook his head. 'No reports of any young children found on their own.'

John's partner was back with the bag of saline and Fliss moved to help prepare Callum for evacuation. Another complete set of vital sign measurements was taken and Fliss noted another slight drop in blood pressure. It was a relief to transfer her small patient to the stretcher, fluids running full bore, a fresh supply of oxygen and full batteries in the monitoring equipment.

'They may be able to take two patients in the chopper,' John said. 'Who's next on the priority list?'

'I've got two more who'll need evacuation to hospital as soon as possible,' Fliss responded, 'but I don't want Callum held up. The others could go by road.'

'Status?'

'Three. They're both in mild hypovolaemic shock but stable. Roger has sustained an arterial injury to his arm and Maria, who's on the bed in the surgery, has a compound fractured femur and has just given birth.'

John's jaw dropped. 'You've been busy!'

'I had some help earlier.' Fliss lowered her voice as she tucked a blanket around Callum. 'Do you know what's happening outside, John? Is it really over?'

'They wouldn't have let us across the bridge if it wasn't. It's been as frustrating as hell, waiting over there. Did you hear the shoot-out?'

Fliss nodded.

'They caught the gang members, who surrendered, but the other guy with the gun – Darren someone?'

'Blythe. Darren Blythe.' Her nod was curt this time.

Fliss was holding her breath as she waited for more information.

'He got cornered, apparently. Did his best to shoot his way out and there's a rumour that one of the SERT members was hit, but then Darren turned the gun on himself when he realised he wasn't going to get away.'

Fliss barely heard the last part of John's account. 'Who was hit?'

'Don't know. There's a few guys apparently not accounted for yet. It's a bit chaotic out there right now, with people trying to find each other and all the extra emergency service personnel coming in.'

John picked up the handle at the end of the stretcher. 'Let's get going.'

But the access to the door of the medical centre was blocked as more people arrived. Two were in police uniform. The third man was Bob Johnston, the father of the twins. He must have finally persuaded the authorities to let him in to find his son, and the strain was still obvious. He seemed to have aged ten years since the last time Fliss had seen him.

'Oh my God! Is that Callum?' Bob dropped to his knees beside the head of the stretcher. 'Cal? It's okay, son. Dad's here.'

Callum stirred. His eyes fluttered open. 'Dad?'

Bob had tears running unheeded down his face. He stroked back the blond hair from his son's forehead. 'Mummy's waiting for you over the bridge, Cal. She can't wait to see you. Where's Cody?'

But Callum's eyes closed again and his face folded into lines of distress. 'Hurts, Dad...'

'What hurts, buddy?' Bob waited only a heartbeat for the response that didn't come. His gaze flicked towards Fliss and she could feel his fear like a solid object. 'How bad is it?'

'We're moving him now. He needs surgery, Bob. He's got a bullet wound in his abdomen and we think it clipped a rib and affected his breathing. He's lost a fair bit of blood.'

'Oh... *God!*'

'He's been relatively stable but what he really needs now is to get to hospital and a surgeon.' Fliss put her hand on Bob's shoulder. She couldn't comfort him by offering promises she had no way of keeping, but she had to say something more. 'You can go with him, Bob. It'll help if you're there.'

Callum's father was struggling with tears again as he stood up and moved back to allow the stretcher to move. 'But where's Cody?' he asked hoarsely. 'How did Callum even get here?'

'We don't know where Cody is yet.' Fliss nodded at John and his partner, who began to wheel the stretcher away. 'It was Jack who saved Callum, though, I do know that.'

'Jack?'

Fliss nodded, her gaze unconsciously travelling to the shrouded figure close by.

'You mean Jack Henley? The old codger with one arm who lives at the top of our road?'

Fliss nodded again, sadly this time. Was that how Jack was going to be remembered? As a rather eccentric old-timer who spent too much time at the local pub?

'My oldest customer,' Roger put in. 'Probably my best one.'

Fliss found herself smiling. 'Mine, too.'

'I did wonder why he wasn't down at the Hog tonight.'

'He was sick,' Fliss told them. 'I was doing a home visit to Jack when this all started. We heard the shots and saw Callum hiding under the hedge, but when I decided I had to get back to the surgery, Jack insisted on going the more dangerous route so he could help Callum.'

'He *carried* him? All the way here? How the hell did he manage that with one arm?' Bob was watching the stretcher carrying his son disappear through the narrow doorway.

'He just did,' Fliss said quietly.

'Is that what gave him the heart attack?' Roger asked soberly.

'It wouldn't have helped,' Fliss said, 'but it might have happened anyway. Maybe we're just lucky he lasted long enough to save Callum.'

She caught Bob's gaze as he turned back just before stepping through the door. 'And he did save Callum, Bob. There's no way he would have survived until now if Jack hadn't got him here.'

'The man's a bloody hero,' Roger stated.

John poked his head back through the door. 'We're ready to roll,' he informed Fliss. 'There's another ambulance coming for your other patients. We've got a doctor waiting at the chopper but do you want to come with Callum?'

Detective Inspector Ross Stringer had been standing to one side over the last few minutes, alternately speaking to his partner and into his portable radio. He had clearly been keeping tabs on what was happening in the medical centre, however, because he spoke up before Fliss had time to respond to the paramedic's query.

'We'll need a statement from you, Dr Slade, before you go anywhere.'

'I'm not going anywhere just yet,' Fliss said. 'I'll stay here until we can evacuate Maria and Roger.'

And Jack. How long would her old friend have to stay here until arrangements could be made? Long enough for the word of Jack's heroic last act to spread through the whole community, perhaps? Would the people of Morriston gather at some point in the near future and honour the contribution Jack had made? Would they see past outward appearances and obvious vices to applaud the man he really had been?

Blinking hard, Fliss focused on the open door of the medical centre for a moment to collect herself. The ambulance carrying Callum and his father moved away and its headlights illuminated a group of people being shepherded from their homes by uniformed police. A woman – Mrs Carson, probably – was crying. Clutching the edges of a blanket draped around her shoulders to pull it more tightly around herself.

Another knot of people was moving in the opposite direction. More uniforms and another civilian in their midst. A male, striding purposefully towards the medical centre.

'Ben!'

'Who's that?' Ross sounded suspicious. He moved to block the entranceway.

'He's the husband of my other patient, Maria.'

'*Ben!*' Maria's cry could be heard all the way into the street.

'*Maria!*' Ben wasn't about to be stopped, even by the broad, uniformed chest blocking the entrance. 'Let me in, man! That's my *wife* in there!'

'He broke through the cordon on the north side,' one of the accompanying police officers told Ross. 'We only caught up with him down the end of this street and it seemed reasonable to let him check to see if his wife was here.'

Ross muttered something about the operation turning into a circus, but he stood back to allow Ben access and then ordered his companions back to their posts. Fliss followed Ben across the waiting room and into the surgery. Maria was smiling... and crying.

Ben stopped just inside the door, taking in the astonishing sight of Maria – her leg in the long splint and her arms holding a now peacefully sleeping newborn baby.

'It's a boy,' Maria told her husband shakily. 'We've got a son, Ben, and he's fine.'

'Are you?' Ben strode towards the bed, reaching out carefully to cradle as much of Maria in his arms as he could. 'Are *you* fine, darling?'

'I am now.' But Maria was still sobbing. 'It's been awful, Ben. I've been so worried about you and the girls. Where are they? Are they safe?'

'Of course. There's a very nice policewoman looking after them. I took the truck down to where they'd closed off the road and just waited, but when they still wouldn't let me in after they heard it was over, I came in anyway – on foot.' Ben grinned. 'I had to run fast. Just as well I'm so fit, isn't it?'

'I have to go to the hospital, Ben.' Maria clung to her husband. 'Fliss says I need an operation on my leg. I'm... scared.'

'I'll be there with you, darling. It'll be all right.' Ben's head swivelled so that he could see Fliss. 'It *will* be all right, won't it, Doc?'

Fliss smiled. 'Yes.' The joy of seeing at least part of this family reunited added warmth to her tone. 'Maria needs the wound in her leg cleaned up properly and the bone damage will need sorting out by an orthopaedic specialist.'

'How did it happen?'

'I got shot.' The tension of the long night was still taking its toll on the young mother, and she dissolved into tears again.

'What, in *here*?' Ben sounded appalled and he looked around as though fearful someone else was present in the surgery who might try and harm his family.

'It was down in the cemetery,' Fliss told him.

'What?'

'I saw him,' Maria said hoarsely. 'I was walking up from the shop when I heard the shooting and then I saw him... Darren, I think... running towards me. And there was someone else. I was trying to hide and I ran into the cemetery, but they were shooting at each other.'

Maria took a gasping breath. 'I thought they were going to kill me and it was so dark and I was too scared to call out and... and I couldn't move and...'

'How did you get here?'

'Angus found me. He carried me.'

'Who the hell is Angus?'

'He's a paramedic,' Fliss supplied. 'He works with the police in a specialist emergency response team. He's... an old friend of mine.'

'More than a friend.' Maria took another shaky breath and sniffed hard, clearly trying to collect herself. 'I saw the way you two kept looking at each other when you thought nobody could see you.'

Fliss was quite willing to give Maria some distraction from her own predicament for a moment or two.

'Yes,' she said quietly. 'He was a lot more than a friend.'

'Maybe some good will come out of all this,' Maria said. 'And you two can get back together.'

The hope was too much to allow its gleam to chase away any more of the darkness. What if it came to nothing? If Fliss didn't allow herself to hope, she wouldn't have to cope with the devastation of it being in vain. Wouldn't have to pick herself up and make the effort of starting her life again. She'd been through all that too recently. And not all that successfully if the raw emotions she had experienced tonight were any indication.

'Some good has already come out of it,' she responded. 'You've got a gorgeous, healthy baby.'

They all looked at the infant as Ben took him in his arms and admired the newest addition to his family.

'What will happen to him while I'm in hospital?' Maria asked anxiously.

'I'll be there,' Ben said. 'I'll take care of him.'

'But what about the girls?'

'I reckon Mrs McKay would look after them for us.'

'How long will I have to be in hospital, Fliss?'

'I can't say. It will depend on what sort of damage they find. You're going to need a lot of help at home for a while, too.'

Another ambulance crew was crowding into the small surgery now. Maria was transferred gently onto a stretcher.

'Can my husband come with me in the ambulance? And my baby?'

The ambulance officer turned to Fliss. 'Haven't you got another patient on the priority list?'

'I can wait.'

Fliss was amazed to turn and find Roger on his feet, his arm on the doorframe for support.

'You stay with Maria, Ben,' he said. 'And don't worry about the girls. We'll see they're well looked after.'

His reassurance didn't seem to be enough.

'Wait!' Maria's command stopped the forward movement of her stretcher. 'I can't go just yet.'

'Why not?'

'I need to talk to Angus. To say thank you.'

'Who's Angus?' the paramedic asked. 'And where is he?'

Maria looked up at Fliss, waiting for her to explain, and Fliss almost smiled wearily. The paramedic had echoed a question she seemed to be hearing rather frequently tonight.

Who was Angus?

Only the man she loved with all her heart and soul. The man she wanted to spend the rest of her life with. To share every possible moment they were lucky enough to have together.

And right now she had no idea where he was. Or whether he was still safe. She had to find out and she could only do that once she had discharged her immediate responsibilities.

Fliss cleared her throat. 'I'll find Angus,' she promised Maria. 'And I'll pass on your thanks.'

She would. It was the perfect reason to talk to him again when the tension of this night was well over. When there was no need for either of them to shy away from personal issues that might distract them from the jobs they needed to do.

'You need to go now, Maria. And you need to go as soon as possible, Roger. You've both got wounds that need stitching from experts and you both need treatment for blood loss.' She turned back to the paramedic. 'We could fit everyone into your ambulance, yes?'

'You coming with us, Dr Slade?'

'We need a statement from you.' Ross Stringer was still standing just outside the medical centre.

'Later,' Fliss told him.

She wasn't going to be delayed if she could help it. The rescue base setup in the domain on the other side of the bridge would be the most likely place to find Angus, wouldn't it? The SERT members probably had to meet for some kind of a debrief after an incident like this. There would be plenty of other pre-hospital emergency medical supplies and personnel available as well. Was that why the injured member of the squad had not been brought to the medical centre?

'I have to go,' Fliss said firmly. 'I need to stay with my patients until they're transferred to the care of other medics.'

'I'll come with you, then,' the detective said.

'Someone needs to stay here.'

'Oh?'

Fliss looked over her shoulder, her glance an eloquent reminder that the surgery was not yet emptied of people.

Ross looked resigned. 'Someone will stay.' He raised an eyebrow at Fliss. 'I'm getting the distinct impression that you're trying to avoid giving me that statement I need.'

'I've just got other things on my mind right now. Like my patients.'

And finding Angus.

'Fair enough. Let's get them all sorted, then.'

The ambulance was overcrowded and had to move very slowly on its short journey to the outskirts of Morriston, its wheels crunching through the shingle of the unsealed streets.

Maria was on one stretcher, holding her baby, and Roger was lying on the other stretcher. Fliss perched on the seat tucked in at the head of Maria's stretcher and Ben sat up front with the driver. Ross and the other crew member were standing in the aisle, keeping their balance by hanging on to the rail designed for IV fluid clips.

Fliss glanced through the square windows on the back doors as they pulled away. They were framing her small medical centre and she realised that she could see the outline of her cottage without the aid of artificial illumination. The inky cover that had cloaked Morriston and the horror of the longest night of her life was finally giving way to the first probing fingers of light from a new day.

It was almost over.

10

The inhabitants of Morriston were gathered on the domain.

Vehicles and tents providing bases for the emergency services covered much of the grassy area. The citizens of the small town were vastly outnumbered by rescue personnel and a huge contingent of media was now adding to the light, noise and general confusion.

Angus McBride was inside the largest tent, which was serving as a mobile first-aid station. He had just seen the ambulance carrying young Callum arrive but had still been too out of breath to chase it when it had closed its doors a few seconds later, having collected a waiting doctor. He could still see the vehicle, its beacons flashing, as it made its way to the helicopter that waited, its rotors turning as it idled, on standby for a rapid take-off.

Exhaustion was ebbing now. Chased away by a few minutes of rest and easily replaced by the burning desire to move again. To go back in the direction he had just come from. To go and find Fliss and make sure she was safe.

'You okay, mate?'

'A hell of a lot better now I've got some of that jungle juice on board.' Seth looked up at his colleague. 'I thought you were supposed to carry stuff like morphine for when we got mown down in the line of duty.'

'I'd used it up on the woman with the broken leg, remember? Maria?'

'Oh, yeah. You've done your bit carrying the wounded tonight, haven't you?'

'Nobody that weighed anything like as much as you do.'

'My apologies.' The narcotic pain relief had restored much of Seth's good humour. 'I could have walked, you know. I seem to remember it was you that insisted on playing the hero.'

'Walked? On that ankle? I don't think so.'

'The bullet didn't even come out the other side. It was only a ricochet. My ankle probably isn't even broken.'

'It's broken all right. You know as well as I do how dangerous a high-velocity bullet is when it bounces. You're bloody lucky it was your ankle and not your head.'

'Yeah. Did you see the holes left by the bullets that went into that water tank instead of bouncing off?'

'I sure did. It looked like some attraction at a water park.' Angus could hear the sound of the helicopter taking off. Had Fliss gone in the helicopter with the other doctor assigned the care of the most critically injured victim from this incident? Craning his neck, he could see outside where the flap of the tent had been pinned back. The ambulance was coming back.

'Got to go,' he informed Seth. 'You'll be well looked after by these guys.'

'They've done a better job than you so far,' Seth agreed with a grin. 'I feel great.'

Angus shook his head as he moved away, but had to pause at Seth's quiet call.

'Hey... Gus?'

'Yeah?'

'Thanks, mate.'

'You're welcome. All part of the service.'

Assisting his colleague after he'd been hit in that final show-down *had* simply been part of his job. A job that Angus felt quite confident he was leaving behind as he strode out of the tent. The thought did not provoke any regret, however. If this was the way forward so that he and Fliss could be together, then he would never have any regrets.

Angus tapped on the driver's window of the ambulance as the vehicle stopped outside the tent.

'Did Dr Slade go on that chopper with the boy?'

'No.' John gave Angus a curious glance. 'Fliss stayed at the medical centre. She's still got some patients she's waiting to evacuate.'

'You going back there, then?'

'Nope. Another truck went in to get them. I've got an injured cop to take to the airport. There's a fixed-wing plane waiting to transfer him to Christchurch.'

Angus nodded but said nothing. He was looking around him now, wondering if there were any other vehicles that could hasten his journey back to Morriston's medical centre.

There were too many people. Too much noise. A second heli-copter was coming in to land and a convoy of army trucks rumbled past. He could go and find his squad and ask for assistance but the likelihood of being detained for some kind of debrief made it an unattractive option.

Angus did not want to be detained. When a television camera and a determined-looking young woman holding a microphone made a beeline for his position, a plan of action was easy to formulate.

'Sorry,' Angus told the reporter. 'Can't stop.'

He turned in the direction of the bridge, but the army vehicles were blocking the access, forcing Angus to take a longer route. He missed seeing the arrival of a second ambulance into the domain as he shouldered his way through the portions of the crowd he couldn't avoid. As soon as it began to thin out and he got out of the gates and within sight of the bridge, Angus broke into a steady jog.

* * *

A helicopter was touching down as the ambulance inched its way through an astonishingly large crowd of people. Having passed a wall of army trucks, it stopped outside the first-aid station where a medical team was waiting to take over the care of its passengers.

Fliss was kept busy with a detailed handover until both Maria and Roger were comfortably settled, having been reassessed prior to their journey to hospital. She went with them to the helicopter and then waited until it took off. The blast of air whipped strands of hair across her face, but she could see Ben waving from his seat beside the pilot.

She waved back. Then she pushed aside the hair obscuring her vision and turned towards the crowd in the domain. Angus had to be somewhere close by.

There were uniforms everywhere. Ordinary police uniforms, the black outfits of the armed-offender squads and here and there the distinctive SERT colours. They were all tall, solid men and each time Fliss caught sight of one, her heart pounded with anticipation. But each time, as she got closer, she could see that none of them was Angus.

They would know where he was, though, wouldn't they? Her attempt to get close enough to speak to one of his colleagues was thwarted more than once.

First it was by a distraught woman that Fliss barely recognised as the mother of the Johnston twins.

'They haven't found him yet, have they?'

'Cody? Not as far as I've heard. I'm sorry, Jenny.'

'They won't let me go and look.'

'There must be a small army of people looking by now.' Fliss tried to sound reassuring. 'They'll find him soon.'

'I should have gone with Callum, but how could I? One of us had to stay for Cody.'

'Of course you did. I know how hard this is for you, Jenny. I wish I could do more to help.'

'Are you going back over the bridge? To the medical centre?'

'I... um...' Fliss wanted to stay where she was. It was the most likely place she was going to find Angus in a hurry.

'If you do, you could watch out for Cody. I can't understand why he wasn't with Callum. They're never more than spitting distance apart, those two.'

Fliss put her arm around Jenny, leading her towards the Red Cross tent where she knew the twins' mother would get the support she needed. Her ordeal was far from over.

Fliss had her own unfinished business – if only she could get on with it.

The media had other ideas.

'Are you Morriston's doctor? Can you tell us about what's been happening?'

'How many people have been killed?' A microphone appeared from nowhere, too close to her face for comfort.

'What kind of injuries did people have?'

'How serious were they?'

Fliss put up a hand to shield her eyes from the spotlight beside the television camera pointing at her face.

'You'll have to talk to the police,' she told them. 'I'm really not in a position to make any comment at this stage.'

'But you were there. We want to hear what you have to say.'

Fliss shook her head. She waved towards the huge truck that was providing the base for the police.

'Go over there,' she told the reporters firmly. She kept her arm out to push her way through the knot of people. 'I have to go. Excuse me.'

The police truck was where she should have been heading herself. She had promised Ross Stringer that she would be back when the helicopter had taken off, in order to provide the statement he was still waiting for regarding her version of the night's events. She could see him over there now, his head turning as he scanned the crowd, probably looking for her.

Fliss wasn't ready to sit down and talk to anybody just yet. Or maybe one person... if she could find him.

She ducked past an empty ambulance and made a beeline for a SERT member.

'Where's Angus?' she asked. 'Angus McBride?'

The man was smiling at her. 'Hey, you're Fliss, aren't you? Are you okay?'

The warmth of the greeting was confusing. Fliss peered up at the man.

'I'm Tom,' he said. 'Another paramedic, like Gus. I met you a while back at a station barbecue, remember?'

Fliss could see past the camouflage crayon now. 'Tom,' she said delightedly. 'Of course I remember. You must know where Angus is. I really need to talk to him.'

But Tom shook his head. 'I haven't seen him since we got split up at the start of this operation. I'm not even sure if he and Seth made it to the rendezvous. All hell broke loose there for a while.'

'I know. I heard it.'

'He was having trouble with his radio earlier. That might still be causing problems.'

'Seth's radio was working. They'd still be together, wouldn't they?'

'Should be.'

Angus had been prepared to let his partner go without him, though, hadn't he? He'd been willing to break protocol to stay with her.

Tom could see her anxiety. 'Don't worry,' he said. 'They're probably on their way back. They'll turn up soon enough.'

Soon wasn't good enough. Fliss wanted to see Angus *now*. To reassure herself that he was safe.

The tap on her shoulder made her jump.

'You got time for that statement now?' Ross asked.

'Ah...' Fliss looked longingly at the gates of the domain. At the road leading to the bridge and back into Morriston. She wanted to run across that bridge and through the narrow dusty streets. Calling for Angus and searching until she found him.

'Dr Slade?' Another police officer joined Detective Inspector Stringer. A man who had even more decoration on the epaulettes of his shirt.

'Yes?'

'You're the only doctor we have available on scene right now. Could you come with me, please?'

'Of course. Is someone hurt?'

'Dead,' the man said succinctly. 'We need some paperwork done for confirmation before we seal the scene for later investigation.'

Fliss shivered as a chill snaked down her spine. She was too frightened to ask whether this had anything to do with the missing SERT members.

'Constable Bowden will take you in,' she was told. 'We've got a car waiting.'

'Make sure she gets brought straight back,' Ross said. 'I've got an interview lined up with Dr Slade.'

Fliss could say nothing.

She couldn't do this.

She *had* to do this.

She had to know. This waiting and not knowing was unbearable.

With her heart in her mouth and her knees weak enough to make her stumble on her first step, Fliss followed her new police escort.

Back into Morriston.

Back to find out whether she still had any hope of the future she wanted.

* * *

The protocol for confirming cessation of life was merely a formality.

Nobody could have survived a head wound like that.

Self-inflicted.

Whatever – probably drug-induced – demons that had led Darren Blythe to help prolong the terror suffered by the inhabitants of Morriston for nearly twelve hours had been silenced for ever.

Fliss did what she had to do, checking for any signs of life. Of course, she found nothing. She filled in and signed the required paperwork and handed it to the officer in charge of the scene. Then she stepped out from the tarpaulin screen erected to prevent the image of Darren's body making its way to the front page of some newspaper.

Constable Bowden was waiting for her. 'You all right?'

Fliss gave a single curt nod. What a silly question.

'You look awfully pale.'

'I don't like suicides.' Fliss swallowed with difficulty. 'In fact, I'd appreciate a few minutes to myself if that's okay.'

She could see her escort debating whether to remind her of the interview she was supposed to be taken straight back to.

'It's a personal thing,' she added quietly. 'My mother committed suicide.'

The police officer looked shocked. 'That's awful!' he exclaimed. 'I'm so sorry.'

'It was a long time ago.' Fliss was amazed it had been so easy to tell a stranger when it had only been a few hours ago that she had talked about it for the first time. And she had managed to say it without being overwhelmed by grief. Or guilt.

Something huge had changed tonight.

It felt like a new chapter of her life had been opened.

A fresh, clean page to start on.

'Take all the time you need,' Constable Bowden told her. 'I'll wait for you here.'

* * *

The conclusion to the incident at Morriston had occurred near the bottom of the hill that led to Jack's house. Not far from the smouldering remains of the cottage that had been Darren's home.

Fliss saw the volunteer firemen working to dampen down the hot spots. Had the fire been an accident? Or had Darren thought he was somehow covering his trail and that destroying his dwelling would keep him hidden from the men he'd had good reason to be so afraid of?

It was a question unlikely to ever be answered and maybe it needed to be left in what was, thankfully, becoming the past.

With an unconscious resolve to move on, Fliss began walking away from the remnants of the fire.

Away from the activity as crime-scene tapes were being stretched between trees to contain the area where Darren had died.

If she walked a little way up the hill towards Jack's house, Fliss knew she would get a good view of the sea. With some distance from the sounds of the people getting started on the clean-up phase of the night's horror, she might be able to hear the wash of surf on the pebble beach below and find a moment or two of peace.

Nobody had yet taped the section of the street where two small bicycles lay abandoned. The forlorn sight was enough to stop Fliss in her tracks as she remembered the anguish in Jenny Johnston's eyes. Fliss bowed her head for a moment, hoping desperately that Jenny's missing son would be found soon. Unscathed. And that her injured son would make it through the surgery he was probably undergoing right now.

'Fliss?'

The call was so quiet, Fliss thought she had imagined it. A memory from another hope that nothing could suppress. A voice she had been desperate to hear again.

Her eyes flew open. She *hadn't* imagined the call. Angus was climbing the hill. He looked out of breath, as though he had been running for some time, but he wasn't running now. He seemed almost hesitant – unsure of whether his presence would be welcome.

'Gus!'

Fliss had been hoping for a moment of peace in solitude, but being alone was the last thing she really wanted. It was far,

far better to forgo a peaceful calm in favour of this flood of pure joy. Sheer relief to see that Angus was safe and an overwhelming gratitude that she was being given the chance to say the things she would have regretted leaving unsaid for the rest of her life.

Angus had stopped now. Fliss could see a muscle in his jaw twitching and when he spoke, his voice was raw with emotion.

'I've been looking for you, Fliss.'

'I'm here.'

'You are.' Angus was smiling. That wide smile Fliss loved so much with those delicious upward curls at the corners. But Fliss could also see tears in his eyes.

'I was looking for you, too,' she said softly.

'Were you?'

'Yes.' Fliss ignored the tears she could feel gathering in her own eyes. 'There was something I wanted to tell you. Something I should have said a lot earlier tonight.'

'What was it?'

'That I love you.' Fliss had to choke back a sob. 'I always have, Gus, and... and I always will.'

Fliss had no idea whether it was her that stepped towards Angus or whether he strode forwards to catch her in his arms. It didn't matter.

All that mattered was that they were close enough to touch. To cling to each other tightly enough to feel the beat of each other's hearts. To taste the tears that mingled as their lips met.

It was not a gentle kiss and it was as brief as it was intense, but it carried a depth of emotion that Fliss would never forget.

And somewhere in that physical contact was a reminder of what they had once shared and a promise that it could be even better from now on.

Precious.

That unspoken promise had to be enough for now. This was certainly neither the time nor place to rekindle passion.

Fliss pulled back from Angus reluctantly. 'I have to go back to the domain,' she said. 'There's a police officer who's waiting to interview me.'

'I should be there as well.' Angus sighed agreement but wasn't releasing his hold on Fliss. 'I haven't been officially stood down yet so I'm probably in trouble for going off to look for you.'

'How much trouble?'

Angus smiled. 'It doesn't matter. I'm going to resign from the squad in any case.'

'What?' Fliss was shocked. '*Why?*'

'I've had a chance to reassess my life in the last few hours. My job broke us up, Fliss.' Angus stroked his fingers gently down her cheek. 'I'm not about to risk that happening again.'

'No.' Fliss shook her head. 'You love what you do. You're not the only one who's had a chance to think about things, Gus. Last night I realised what it's like to be waiting for someone like you to come and help. What you do is special. It takes far more courage than most people have. I'm *proud* of you.'

'You should be proud of yourself,' Angus responded softly. 'You've faced far worse things than I ever have.'

'Only when I've had no choice. You were right. I ran away when things got difficult between us.'

'I won't let that happen again. I don't need this job, my love. I need you.'

'And I need you.' Fliss pressed herself closer to the man she loved. '*So* much.'

'We can make it work this time.'

'Yes.'

A single word, but Fliss knew nothing more needed to be said for now. Once-locked doors had been opened between them, thanks to the emotional trauma of what they had both been through in a single night, and what they'd discovered had given them the kind of closeness and understanding that would take them well into the future.

Together.

* * *

One of those doors had provided access to memories that were still surfacing as the sun inched its way higher on the horizon.

When Fliss and Angus managed to separate their physical contact enough to simply hold hands as they started their return to the domain and the duties still required of them, a startlingly vivid memory made Fliss pause and tug Angus to a halt.

'I had a macrocarpa hedge like that around the property I grew up in,' she told Angus.

'Oh?' Fliss couldn't blame Angus for sounding somewhat bewildered by her apparently irrelevant comment.

'They're weird things, macrocarpa hedges,' she continued steadily. 'They look solid from the outside but they have all this dead space around the trunks in the middle.'

She could see the spark of comprehension in those dark eyes, and the lines of exhaustion softened as Angus turned his head to glance at the bicycles lying in the street. Fliss loved Angus for the way he was so prepared to listen... and the way he had no trouble following her line of thought.

'My hedge had this tunnel and you could crawl from one end right to the other.'

'A good place to hide.' The grip on her hand tightened as Angus took a step towards the hedge.

'I stayed in mine for hours once. I was hiding because I was scared of what would happen when Mum found out I'd broken her favourite vase.'

They had to let go of each other's hands to part the branches of the hedge and peer into the dusty space inside.

'Cody?' Angus called. 'Are you in here, buddy?'

They worked their way downhill from where the bikes lay.

'Cody?' Fliss called again and again. 'Where are you, love?'

Her hands were scratched. She could smell the pungent oil from crushed needles, and the residue of long-dead vegetation made her cough and sneeze repeatedly. The heat from the gathering sunlight was hot on the back of her neck, and exhaustion made the hedge appear to stretch for miles.

There was no response to any of their calls.

They could find nothing.

Finally nearing the end of the hedge, Fliss stepped back to push tangled strands of hair from her face. She turned to Angus. Was it time to admit defeat and turn away?

But Angus smiled at her. Despite any lack of evidence to the contrary, he still believed in her idea. In her. He wasn't about to give up.

And neither was Fliss.

She parted a new set of branches and poked her head right into the hedge.

'Cody?'

Fliss backed out much faster than she had gone in.

'Fliss? What's wrong, love?'

'I saw something.'

'Cody?'

'I think so.' But Fliss gulped and took another step backwards. 'He's not moving, Gus.'

Angus did more than just part the branches. He bent them and twisted them, oblivious to the damage he was doing to his hands and arms, snapping branches off until he had created a hole large enough to see the small shape of a curled-up child. He knelt down.

'Hey,' Fliss heard him say very gently. 'What's happening, buddy?'

For a long, long moment, Fliss stared at the curved back of the man in front of her as Angus hid Cody from her view.

Then, miraculously, she saw two skinny arms snake themselves around Angus's neck. He wriggled backwards and then stood up, with a small boy blinking sleepily in his arms.

'Are you all right, Cody?' Fliss had to clear her throat. 'Does anything hurt?'

Cody shook his head and then opened his mouth. 'Where's Callum?' he demanded. 'And where's my bike?'

'Your bike's not far away, mate,' Angus told him.

'And Callum's gone for a ride in a helicopter,' Fliss added. 'I know where your mum is, though, and she's going to be very happy to see you.'

Angus smiled over the top of Cody's head. 'And you, Fliss?' he asked quietly. 'Are you very happy?'

Fliss could have drowned in the emotional well she was in right now.

'I don't think I've ever been this happy in my entire life,' she whispered.

'Hmm.'

With a satisfied nod and a look that caressed Fliss with all the love it was possible for one person to offer another, Angus turned to carry Cody back to his mother.

'Me too,' he said.

EPILOGUE

A YEAR LATER…

'It all looks exactly the same.'

'Places like this never really change.'

'Shall we park the car here and walk?'

'I'm not sure that's a great idea, darling.' Angus McBride gave his wife a speculative glance. 'I wouldn't want you going into labour halfway up that hill.'

'I'm weeks away yet.' Fliss patted the huge mound of her belly. 'This is going to be a Christmas present, this baby.'

Angus chuckled. 'Make sure you keep it wrapped up, then.'

They were heading across the bridge now. Into what represented the town centre of Morriston. Where Mrs McKay's general store looked to still be the main competition for the pub in any commercial enterprise here. 'Oh… look!'

'What?'

'The pub.'

'Looks exactly the same to me.'

'They've changed the name.'

Angus gave a huff of laughter. '"Jack's Arms"? Is that meant to be a joke?'

'I suspect it's more of a tribute.'

'But he only had one arm.'

Fliss smiled. 'I reckon they've given him back the lost one.'

'I guess Roger decided to stay on after all.'

'Yeah. I think Jack's funeral gave the whole community the chance to see how special this place is.'

'I wonder how many of them would have turned up for Darren's funeral if it hadn't been up north.'

Fliss was silent for a moment. 'I'm sure he's been forgiven by now. It's not as if he actually killed anyone. The only murders were the Barrett brothers and that was done by the gang affiliates from Christchurch.'

'If Darren had opened his door when they went knocking, it would have saved a whole heap of trouble, though.'

'Would you have opened the door?'

'Not if I'd been up to what Darren had,' Angus admitted with a wry smile. 'He was stupid to have got involved in any drug dealing in the first place.'

'But that's where using leads all too often. Drug habits are expensive.'

'It's all pretty sad, isn't it?' Angus was slowing the car as he looked around. 'Hard to believe that was all a year ago.'

'It's flown past, hasn't it?' Fliss agreed. 'Not surprising, though, when we had so much to get done.'

'Yeah.' Angus sounded smug. 'And the wedding was the best part.'

'It was.' Fliss sighed happily. 'Mind you, hunting for our house was great fun, and I have to confess I've loved being back working in the emergency department.'

'And you've just been made a consultant. You'll miss it while you're on maternity leave.'

'Doubt it. I'll have something far more exciting to keep me busy for a while.'

Angus nodded. 'That's how I've felt about going back to being a road-based paramedic. Anything I've missed out on has been more than made up for by what I've got outside working hours.'

His hand left the steering wheel and rested for a moment on the rounded belly that hid their first child.

'Ooh, he kicked you.' Fliss laid her hand over the top of his. 'Did you feel that?'

'Sure did.'

'I think he's hungry,' Fliss announced. 'Could we stop at the shop for a minute? I've got this really bad craving for ice cream.'

Angus laughed. 'Don't you mean you've got a really bad craving for a bit of gossip?'

'Huh!' Fliss tried to sound indignant but had to join in the chuckle as Angus slowed the car and stopped. He knew her far too well. 'Hey... Gus?'

'Yeah?'

'I love you.'

Angus unclipped his safety belt and leaned over to kiss her. The kind of slow, exquisitely gentle kiss that was a regular feature of any daytime hours they spent together.

'Not half as much as I love you,' he murmured eventually.

'So how come I haven't got my ice cream yet, then?'

'You distracted me.'

'Oh.' Fliss finally tore her gaze away from Angus. 'That will never do. Come on.' She unclipped her safety belt but waited until Angus was ready to help her out of the vehicle. 'I feel like a stranded whale every time I sit down,' she complained.

'Well, you *are* getting pretty fat.'

Fliss narrowed her eyes. 'Just for that, I think I might have two ice creams.'

'That'll help.' Angus kept hold of her hand as they entered the general store, which was just as well because they had a near collision with a small boy who was exiting the premises at speed.

'Callum Johnston,' a female voice yelled. 'Come back here this instant!'

'Hi, Jenny!' Fliss was beaming. 'Great to see that Callum's giving you the run around again.'

Jenny rolled her eyes but smiled as she returned the greeting. She handed two full grocery bags to Callum as he arrived back, and her harassed expression softened noticeably as she ruffled her son's curls.

'Thanks,' she said to Fliss. 'Sometimes I need reminding of just how good it is to have him back to normal.' Callum had ducked away from his mother's caress. He was scowling. 'How come Cody doesn't have to carry bags?'

'You know why.'

'He could carry *one*.'

'No, I can't. It might hurt my good arm and I need that to write with.'

Fliss eyed the cast on Cody's left forearm. 'What have you done to yourself, Cody?'

'I broke my arm,' the seven-year-old said proudly.

'He fell off his bike,' Jenny sighed.

'*He* didn't get to ride in a helicopter,' Callum told Fliss. 'But *I* did.'

'You don't even remember going in the helicopter.'

'Yes, I do.'

'That's not what you said before.'

'Stop arguing,' their mother ordered. 'It's time we got home and made dinner for Dad. I'll have to catch up with you later, Fliss. You'll be around for a while?'

'Absolutely.'

Jenny picked up another two bags. 'I was so pleased to hear the news, by the way. We'll be seeing a bit more of you.'

'There's certainly a bit more of her to see,' Angus put in.

Fliss aimed a kick at his ankle. 'Please excuse my rude husband.'

Jenny was laughing as her gaze dropped. 'When are you due?'

'After Christmas,' Fliss said firmly.

'So's Maria.'

'No! Maria's pregnant *again*?'

'They're aiming for ten kids.' Jenny was peering through the door to see where the twins had disappeared to. 'God knows why. Callum! Cody! Get back here.'

Mrs McKay appeared and made tutting noises. 'Those boys,' she said with fond disapproval.

'They'll be the death of me,' Jenny agreed. 'Gotta go. Good to see you, Fliss. And you, Angus.'

* * *

Mrs McKay was only too happy to take up any slack in passing on the village gossip.

'Maria's quite certain it's going to be another boy. She's going to have her hands full with a new one.'

'She'll cope,' Fliss said. 'Maria's a superwoman.'

'Hmm. She'll have her work cut out this time. She had young Oliver in here today and he was running around, pulling tins off all my shelves.'

'At not quite thirteen months? Good grief, what a monster!'

'It's a blessing that Maria's running just as fast again.'

'So her leg's fine now?'

'Good as new. Took a long time, mind you. She was on those

crutches forever. I kept saying, "Maria, you've got to rest more," but would she listen?'

Angus left the women to enjoy their conversation. He took a trolley and began wandering down the narrow overstocked aisles. They needed supplies for the next few days. As he added cleaning items to the foodstuffs, he wondered how much work would need to be done.

Jack's little house on the hill had been emptied when the estate had finally been sorted out, but it was doubtful whether any cleaning had been done in the six months since then. The process of purchasing the property had been very slow and it had only been last week that he and Fliss had learned of their successful settlement.

Now they had a holiday house. A place to return to each year.

A place to bring their children and give them a taste of a life that would be very different to what the family would have in a larger city.

Angus paused beside a shelf full of fishing tackle. He would take their children fishing one day. And walking in the forests. He'd build a driftwood fire on the beach sometimes and tell them stories.

One day, he might tell them about why this place was so special.

How it had given him – and their mother – the opportunity to find the kind of magic that only the very luckiest of people ever got to find.

Pushing his trolley towards the checkout, he caught sight of the woman he loved, but the joy he always felt on seeing Fliss was tempered with concern. She looked tired and it didn't sound as though Mrs McKay was anywhere near finishing all she wanted to say.

Fliss looked up – as she always seemed to do, even before she could possibly be aware of his approach. The slightly glazed expression on her face changed to one of relief. Her smile was joyous and her eyes told him all he ever needed to know about how much he was loved.

Angus smiled back.

Yes.

He would be able to tell their children with the utmost sincerity that he and Fliss were definitely the luckiest people on earth.

* * *

MORE FROM ALISON ROBERTS

Another uplifting medical romance from Alison Roberts, *Resisting the Surgeon*, is available to order now here:

www.mybook.to/ResistingSurgeonBackAd

ABOUT THE AUTHOR

Alison Roberts is the author of over one hundred romance novels with Mills and Boon, and now writes romance and escapist fiction for Boldwood.

Sign up to Alison Robert's mailing list here for news, competitions and updates on future books.

Visit Alison's website: www.alisonrobertsromance.com

Follow Alison on social media:

facebook.com/rosie.richards.75

instagram.com/alison_roberts_author

ALSO BY ALISON ROBERTS

A Year in France Series

Falling for Provence

From Provence, With Love

Medical Romances

The Doctor's Promise

Doctor Off Limits

The Surgeon's Surprise Baby

A Kiss Before Midnight

Resisting the Surgeon

The Doctor's Second Chance

Boldwood

EVER AFTER

X♡X♡

JOIN BOLDWOOD'S
ROMANCE COMMUNITY
FOR SWEET AND SPICY BOOK RECS WITH ALL YOUR FAVOURITE TROPES!

SIGN UP TO OUR
NEWSLETTER

HTTPS://BIT.LY/BOLDWOODEVERAFTER

Boldwood

Boldwood Books is an award-winning fiction publishing company seeking out the best stories from around the world.

Find out more at www.boldwoodbooks.com

Join our reader community for brilliant books, competitions and offers!

Follow us
@BoldwoodBooks
@TheBoldBookClub

Sign up to our weekly deals newsletter

https://bit.ly/BoldwoodBNewsletter

She was protecting her heart by running away, now he's back in her life and one night is going to change everything.

Dr. Felicity Slade has come to the small coastal town of Morriston for a quieter life - and to distance herself from gorgeous paramedic Angus McBride. She's always known that Angus thrives on the drama and danger of his job with the Specialist Emergency Response Team, and she has never been able to cope with the fear of losing him. So she had to walk away to protect her heart.

But her peace is quickly disrupted when she's plunged into a critical emergency situation and she's immediately out of her depth. But the last thing she expects is for Angus to turn up as part of the medical response team, and her feelings are thrown into confusion (and secretly relief). As they battle through the night to save the lives in their care, it becomes clear that Angus has changed and together they're a really strong team. Even though she feels safe working with him, she knows her heart is still at risk. But could this one night with Angus be what changes everything… forever?

ISBN 978-1-83617-376-2

90000

9 781836 173762

www.boldwoodbooks.com

Designer: Colin Thomas. Images: ©Colin Thomas.

Panic

COLIN SPENCER

'Grotesque . . . macabre . . . brilliant'
Sunday Telegraph